"HIGHLY RECOMMENDED TRIPLE-STARRED STORY"

—NEW YORK HERALD TRIBUNE

A very rich man was dead, violently murdered. A very charming girl was deeply, deeply involved—as was the small town in which the horror took place.

It remained for the clue of the watchman's clock to lead to one of the strangest climaxes in the gory annals of murder.

"THE STORY IS WELL TOLD"

—NEW YORK TIMES

By the Watchman's Clock

Leslie Ford

WILDSIDE PRESS

I

In the little town of Landover the most important thing is Daniel Sutton. Landover College is the next most important. Landover, like the rest of Maryland, measures everybody and everything by two yardsticks. One is Money and the other Age. The conclusion is inevitable. Daniel Sutton is disgustingly rich and the college is exceedingly old. Some people might dispute the matter of priority. There are Marylanders who believe that age is more important than money; but as a rule they are held to be prejudiced. There's certainly no doubt in the minds of practical people that it would be better to be as rich as Daniel Sutton than to be as old as Landover College.

As a matter of fact, to give credit where credit is due, Daniel Sutton has done considerably more for himself than Landover College has ever done for itself.

Daniel Sutton had lived only about sixty-five years. He had none of the fine classic lines of the old buildings on the hill. If anything he was inclined to be short, and to run to Rubens rather than Adam. He was proud, I think, in a half-regretful way, that the evening waistcoat he wore at Yale no longer met by fourteen and one-half inches. There's no doubt he regarded that as more admirable than if it had lapped over that far. One instance was a symbol of success; the other would have been failure, either of Daniel Sutton to provide amply for his inner man, or of the inner man to react comfortably to Daniel Sutton. As it was, they had worked together perfectly. At sixty-five Daniel Sutton, without a twinge except possibly the disturbing knowledge of slightly increased blood-pressure, had multiplied the small estate his father had left him, and was an iron-grey man of vast wealth, with grey hair, myopic grey eyes, a set jaw, and a passion for all things that belonged to Daniel Sutton. More than that, he disliked nearly everybody, and certainly nearly everybody loathed him.

Landover College, on the other hand, had grown lovelier as it grew older. Its lines never altered. Successive generations had done their best with paint and hammer and nails to change the elegant simplicity of Mascham Hall. That phase fortunately is over. Five of the original buildings of the college, all built between 1705 and 1774, are still standing, and are in the finest Georgian manner, simple and lovely. But they are pretty much all that Landover has left of its royal grant of five thousand acres from Queen Anne. More properly the grant might be said to have been made to Abigail Mascham, the Queen's favorite after the fall of Sarah Duchess of Marlborough. Undoubtedly it was the Queen's interest in her favorite rather than in colonial education that prompted the gift.

Abigail Mascham's brother Dick, so the story goes, was in command of a part of her Majesty's troops in the New World. It occurred to him that this continent would be an excellent place for a certain very close connection of the family's, who had taken orders at Cambridge and thereupon had become not only a scandal to the Church of England—which could be put up with—but exceedingly embarrassing to the family. He took it up with his sister, who took it up with the Queen, who promptly agreed that a college in the New World was an ideal place for her favorite's cousin. The necessary grant of lands and money had sent the Vicar to Landover, where he stayed five years and built the college with the help of the local burgesses. No one knows precisely what happened to him after that. He went out one night, quite sober, his servant said, and never returned. The college flourished; it wasn't until after the Civil War that it fell on evil times. Gradually its tobacco fields were sold. Once it had owned most of the land and houses in the little town; they were first heavily mortgaged, then they went under the hammer. This lasted until 1920, when a few old Landoverians got together and said, This has got to stop. The college unfortunately had nothing left, by that time, but the square on which its five buildings had stood surrounded by spreading oaks, tulip poplars and maple trees—the land and the buildings also heavily mortgaged. The job of reclaiming it all looked decidedly hopeless. In fact, as far as its being important in the town at that time is concerned, the college wasn't at all. It was rather in the position of being pretty much of a stepchild. It's because of that that I'm inclined to think everybody here really believes money is more important than age.

So in 1920 the college wasn't important at all, and Daniel Sutton had just come to town. It's just as well that only people can suffer, otherwise I think the little college on the hill must have had a pretty bad time, knowing it had lost everything it ever had, and that the townspeople despised it. So did the students in it, who cut their initials in the mahogany chair rails in the great room in Mascham Hall; to say nothing of

6

the underpaid men who taught in its fine old class rooms and kept cows and raised vegetables on the back campus. Of course, the townspeople despised it, and consequently they sold it decayed foodstuffs at exorbitant rates, and charged it appalling prices for coal that was mostly dust. And like all townspeople of the sort, complained bitterly at having the college quartered on it, very much as if it were a prison and put there to harass the good people of Landover.

That was before Dr. Knox came to make it over. He was drastic. He sent back the first order of bad meat, the first order of stale bread, the first load of poor coal. The people of Landover began to regret the fine old days when their college represented the better traditions of the old Free State. They shook their heads and said, What can you expect? It doesn't surprise us at all! When, as it turned out, some colored boys needed money and sold Ye Gifte Shoppe sign to get it, they shook their heads again. Students did not do such things, they implied, before Dr. Knox in 1920 disturbed the sacred edifice of the old school.

But that is all over now. In fact they are rather inclined to point to the college with some satisfaction, as an example of what enlightened townspeople can accomplish when they put their minds to it. Only a few of the die-hardests still shake their heads and wonder what the world is coming to, if anything. But Mr. Chew, the local leading butcher, says quite plainly that the college is the town's biggest industry. How can a college be an industry? Its meat bill, says Mr. Chew, is bigger than half the town's' put together, if you leave out Mr. Sutton. And obviously you have to leave Mr. Sutton out of all such calculations, because he is very rich and the townspeople of Landover are very poor.

Mr. Sutton's Seaton Hall occupies a piece of Landover something like a large slice of apple pie. One straight side is bounded by York Road, just across the street from the northern half of the college campus. The other straight side is along the full length of King Charles Street, from where it makes a T-Square with York Road down to the edge of Seaton River. 'Seaton River by the way is an arm of the Chesapeake, like the Magothy or the Severn. The grounds of Seaton Hall, laid out in gardens, some formal, others charmingly informal, slope down to the water, the curving outer crust of the piece of pie making an undulating shore several miles long.

When Daniel Sutton came to Landover and bought the Seaton mansion in 1920 it occupied a small plot of ground on York Road extending from Duke of Gloucester Street to

King Charles Street. Duke of Gloucester Street runs from York Road where it joins the State Highway down to the river. There were houses and shops on each side of it, and along the shore were a number of oyster sheds and a small ship-building concern that did a considerable business in Maryland rye and corn whisky. There were also nondescript houses along King Charles Street, and in Bleinheim Road, which intersects King Charles and Duke of Gloucester streets a block down from York Road.

The Seatons had come on evil days since they built their town house on York Road. There's some question in the mind of Mr. Tasker, the librarian and local antiquarian, as to whether their property ever actually ran to the water. However there was no question in Daniel Sutton's mind that if it hadn't it should have, and when he bought the old house from John Seaton he bought all the property in the triangle formed by York Road and King Charles Street. At least he bought all but a plot thirty by seventy-five feet on the corner of Duke of Gloucester Street and York Road. And that plot rose to plague him beyond endurance, and caused him more distress than seems logically possible.

He tore out the houses and the oyster sheds and the shipyard. He tore up the cobblestones and sidewalks on Blenheim Road and Duke of Gloucester Street and erased them completely from the map. He built a ten-foot brick wall, with broken glass firmly set in concrete on the top, along the two edges of his slice of pie, and built a retaining wall along the crust. In two years lilacs and jasmine hung over the brick wall in the spring, and in summer it was covered with trumpet vine and white clematis. Within five years Daniel Sutton's wall might have been there forever, so quickly do people forget old streets and old houses. Even Mr. Tasker had forgotten. Mr. Sutton was the only person who couldn't forget. That was because of those thirty feet along York Road, and old Aunt Charlotte who wouldn't sell them to him.

It was on the morning of April 24th that I came out of my front door and saw Sebastien Baca leaning against the low brick wall that runs around my garden on the corner of York Road and King Charles Street, across from the south wall of Seaton Hall. My house faces the college, I might add, across York Road. I didn't know then that the man was Sebastien Baca. In fact I shouldn't even have known it was April 24th if later events hadn't impressed it on my mind. I'm congenitally unable to keep calendars, stamps or matches in

8

the house. I never know the date and never mail a letter on time.

I was on my way over to see Thorn Carter, Mr. Sutton's niece and an intimate friend of mine. I saw a dark, elegantly dressed man half sitting on my wall, and I hoped for his own sake that the children hadn't left any of their nameless concoctions of mud, berries and garden bugs there for him to mop up with his immaculate light grey flannels. I glanced down at him and noticed that he was absently digging the green moss from between the bricks in the sidewalk, where it isn't much used, with his stick. I remembered at that point that I'd forgot to tell Lillie what sort of a salad we'd have for lunch and went back inside to do it.

When I came out again, ten minutes later, he was still there. It didn't seem strange to me, of course. If you live in a town that's famous for anything, you get quite used to being an unpaid adjunct of the local Chamber of Commerce, especially if you live across the street from a college that has five perfect gems of eighteenth century architecture in plain sight. And if your brick wall is just high enough to make a comfortable perch you quite expect to see people sitting on it. As I say, all you hope is that the children using it as a counter in a store haven't left some frightful, for the moment unnoticeable, mess.

The man turned when I came down the walk to the gate and raised his hat.

"Pardon me, madam. Is that Mr. Daniel Sutton's residence?"

With his stick he indicated the high brick wall across the street, with the heavy clusters of purple and white lilacs hanging over it.

The question was not unusual, but the questioner was decidedly so. In the first place he was definitely foreign. He was above middle height, slim, with clear deep olive skin and brilliant intelligent dark eyes.

"Yes," I said. "It is."

He bowed and thanked me with rather more courtesy than I usually get from the people who use my garden wall as a grand-stand. I crossed the street and continued down York Road under the overhanging lilacs, wondering vaguely how some men managed to look immaculately fresh, as if they'd just come out of the customary bandbox. I was thinking that my husband always managed to look rather mussed, in spite of my efforts, sporadic I'll admit, to keep him pressed. Then I began to wonder what a bandbox was, and forgot all about the olive-skinned foreigner sitting on my wall.

9

II

Tim Healy, the Irish watchman, was parading solemnly back and forth behind the great iron gate of the York Road entrance to Seaton Hall. He hurried to open the side grill for me.

"Good morning, Miss, good morning to you! It's a rare foine day. Miss Thorn'll be as glad to see ye as would the angels themselves, bless ye, Miss!"

Bill Sutton said once that Chicago got the idea of an official greeter from Tim, and I shouldn't be at all surprised. He knew moreover just whom to greet and whom to glower at and turn away, and whom to admit in spite of the fact that the much harassed young man who stands between Daniel Sutton and the world would shortly turn him out again. The family's friends Tim never failed. If the day was bright and fine, and Tim paraded back and forth across the drive, it was a blessing, he assured you, and would be to one of God's very angels, to see you. If the day was bad and Tim limped rheumatically out of his lodge to admit you, he inquired narrowly and with infinite concern into the health of each member of your family. Death and disaster, he regretted, were not far off. Poor old Tim, with his smoked glasses for dark days and his rosy glasses for bright ones. People said he hated Mr. Sutton, but I've never believed it. I've seen them, in the evening, walking back and forth in the side garden, Tim with his black stumpy clay glowing fitfully, Mr. Sutton with a fine cigar making fragrant undertones for it. I don't know what they talked about, but it must have been amusing. Those evenings are the only times I've ever heard Mr. Sutton laugh. Except once. After that I didn't know whether to think it was well or ill for Mr. Sutton to laugh.

In view of all the things that happened later I think it's just as well to sound a warning to all people who've never lived in a college town. It's simply this: never, never forsake the scientific method. In other words, never believe anything you hear until you've examined it closely and found out if it's true or false. Maybe it's because people who live in or around colleges have more imagination, and like the business of creative gossip. I don't know. But if the wife of the professor of Egyptology tells you that Mr. Sutton's wife jumped from the ninth story of a hotel in Paris because she couldn't stand it any longer, don't believe it. I did, for a long time, and viewed Mr. Sutton with fascinated horror. Later I learned that his wife was always delicate and died quite naturally of pneumonia in Paris, Maine.

Thorn Carter and I once started a rumor just for fun and to see what would happen. Before we were through—well, we were two mortified and chastened young women. But that was some years ago. We have more sense now.

I talked with Tim Healy a few minutes about the possibility of rain and whether the summer was to be cool or hot, and went on towards the house.

Seaton Hall itself is a fine old mansion, whose salt glaze bricks have weathered into a deep brownish mauve. The central unit is three stories high with a fine simple doorway and elaborately carved Palladian window and frieze. The wings are separated from the house by two hyphens in the usual Maryland manner. In fact the house is very much like the Brice House in Annapolis, although the people of Landover think it is far more beautiful—now that they've learned to prize their architecture. Rather late, of course, for Daniel Sutton's high brick wall hides the house except through the York Road gate, and there's a ten-foot box hedge across the diameter of the circle of the drive that makes a pretty effectual screen. Very few people now living have actually seen Seaton Hall. Daniel Sutton isn't very gracious about showing it, in fact he won't show it at all.

Lafayette Johnson, the white-haired old Negro who has opened the door at Seaton Hall for as many years as he can rightly remember, opened it now and grinned broadly.

"Mornin', Miss. How *is* you, Miss? How's the Doctor, and how's the children?"

That was Lafayette's formula, never varied rain or shine. With fine darkey tact he called all the instructors at Landover, from the youngest assistant in Chemistry just out of Johns Hopkins to the president himself, Doctor without prejudice. That he called all the students Doctor too, grinning joyfully at his jest, was fair enough, and maybe he didn't realize how finely ironic it was.

One's reply was as set as Lafayette's greeting.

"Morning, Lafayette. I'm fine. It's a lovely day. He's fine and so are the children. How are you?"

"That's good, Miss. I'm tolable. Miss Thorn's upstairs, Miss."

I went up to Thorn's sitting room and went in.

"Hello," she said. She threw the book she was reading on

11

the floor and drew her feet under her to make room for me at the other end of the sofa.

"See Uncle Dan on the way up?" she asked.

"No. Why?"

She shrugged her shoulders.

"Thought you might have," she said indifferently, and added, "he's on the rampage again. You're apt to run into him in the oddest places."

"What's the matter?" I asked, not particularly alarmed, for Daniel Sutton's rampages were nothing new.

She didn't answer me at once, she just sat there tearing into bits a piece of notepaper she'd taken out of her pocket. She seemed unhappy about something, but I couldn't believe it was her uncle, for she, like the rest of his family, takes his peculiarities with inscrutable calm.

I waited for her to speak, watching the sun play on her bent dispirited head, bringing out auburn and gold lights in her wavy chestnut hair. I was a little surprised when I saw a tear fall and make a bright wet spot on her brown arm.

Thorn Carter is about twenty-four, and ordinarily irresistibly alive and gay. In the eight years I'd known her I'd never seen her more than momentarily low. She's not pretty, except that she has beautiful hair, lovely dark brown eyes, and skin rather like the luminous texture of a very fresh egg— not a white one but a delicate ivory-colored one. Thorn Carter *isn't* pretty, but sometimes she's beautiful. And sometimes she looks pretty much like something that's been out in the rain all night. Her face is intelligent and so are her eyes. She's quite different from Susan Atwood, who's her Aunt's ward and lives at Seaton Hall too.

"It's about Franklin," she said, brushing the tears out of her eyes with the back of her hand, very much as a child would do. She looked nearer seventeen then than twenty-four.

"What's he done?" I asked patiently.

Franklin is Dr. Knox's son and a rising young Baltimore lawyer. The Suttons and the Knoxes are very close friends, and have been ever since they came in the same year to Landover.

"He hasn't done anything except ask me to marry him, and Uncle seems to think it's a crime. But that's not what's the matter with him—that's what's the matter with *me*."

She looked up with a sudden smile, her old spirit breaking through for a moment.

I'm afraid I'm not patriarchial enough to be terribly impressed by parents, uncles and guardians.

12

"I don't see what objections your uncle has in the first place," I said a little shortly. "And second, both you and Franklin are old enough to know your own minds."

"Precisely what Uncle Dan says."

She lighted a cigarette and tossed the matches to me.

"Well?" It was my turn to shrug.

"Exactly."

Thorn stared wretchedly at the cascade of pink and white magnolia blossoms just outside the window. "Don't let me stand in your way, my dear," she recited, "if you want to be a fool like your mother. Go right ahead, marry a penniless lawyer when young Fairweather has money enough to provide for you. Go right ahead. But don't count on me for anything. I think I'd better make that clear to Franklin. It wouldn't be fair to let him in for anything."

She gave a perfect imitation of Daniel Sutton's unpleasant sharp precise clipped speech.

"Well, why not?" I asked. "You haven't any doubt about what Franklin would say. I'm not sure it mightn't do your uncle a lot of good to hear it."

Her head was lying back against the cushions in the corner of the sofa. She moved it dejectedly from side to side in weary dissent.

"It's not that," she said. "But I won't have him humiliated. It was hard enough for him to ask me, just for that reason— and I won't have it, Martha, I won't have it."

"That's up to you."

"Oh but you don't know what he's like. Uncle Dan I mean. It's all very well to talk, but you don't have to live here with him. You've no notion how horrible he can be without ever raising his voice. He's always decent to you. He says you're the only woman in Landover who's got a lick of sense. But you ought to see what he's like to everybody else. You don't know him, Martha."

I didn't tell her that I'd heard enough about Daniel Sutton from people who did know him. I don't think Thorn herself knew how everybody in town and everybody at the college, for that matter, loathed him. He'd always been charming to me, and I must say I liked him immensely, with reservations, probably for just that reason. However, there was no use talking with Thorn about it.

"If that's the matter with you, what's the matter with Mr. Sutton?" I inquired peaceably.

She groaned wearily and punched a cushion violently into shape and out again.

"Oh Lord!" she said. "It's Aunt Charlotte again."

"Again?"

She nodded.

"Same old thing. He couldn't get her out ten years ago for two hundred dollars, and he can't get her out for ten thousand dollars now. But that's not it—not quite."

Anyone who's lived in Landover knows the story of Daniel Sutton, multimillionaire, and Charlotte Hawkins, Landover's only living slave. It's a fine example of the gnat and the elephant, although physically Aunt Charlotte is much nearer being the elephant. Long before the Seatons began to go down in the world Aunt Charlotte was Miss Abigail Seaton's colored mammy. Miss Abigail's mother died of galloping consumption after returning from a ball at the Mayhews at London Town one Christmas Eve. Miss Abigail was two years old and Aunt Charlotte was fifteen or so. That was in 1845, when the Seatons still owned most of the county and were people of importance in the state. After the Civil War the Seaton fortunes declined, but when Anthony Seaton died in 1870 he was able to leave the house and grounds to his daughter Abigail and the tobacco plantation to his son. Abigail also died of quick consumption four years later, and left house and grounds to her brother's eldest son, with the exception of a small plot thirty feet long and seventy feet deep on the corner of York Road and Duke of Gloucester Street, where Aunt Charlotte's cabin stood. That she left to Aunt Charlotte and her heirs forever, and there Aunt Charlotte still lived, earning her living by running a small cook shop. Her devilled crabs were famous; many a white person in Maryland wouldn't think of coming to Landover without stopping for them, or oysters and ham, at Aunt Charlotte's whitewashed cottage on York Road. Consequently Aunt Charlotte had done better, comparatively, than the Seatons. She paid her taxes while theirs were in arrears, and when they sold their house and land, and everyone else between King Charles Street and the river sold his to Daniel Sutton, Aunt Charlotte refused flatly to sell hers. It was the only inch of all that land that wasn't mortaged up to the hilt. Aunt Charlotte kept her land and her cabin in which Miss Abigail's picture, a lock of her, and a copy of her will in the wiry handwriting of fifty years ago were framed together and hung over the dresser in the parlor. Aunt Charlotte also had money in the bank and was a respected charter member of a flourishing Burying Society. In all she was as prosperous as anyone in Landover—more so than most, because her needs and her wants coincided and her income was ample for both.

Mr. Sutton had offered her two hundred dollars for her

cabin in 1921. In 1922 he offered three hundred. He was not particularly perturbed in those years, because Aunt Charlotte was sick most of the winter of 1922. She was then ninety-one years old and it was obvious to Mr. Sutton that she could hardly last out the winter. He closed up Duke of Gloucester Street, built his wall to each boundary of Aunt Charlotte's thirty feet and left the intervening space confidently to time. Aunt Charlotte's heir was a worthless old Negro of sixty-some years who would sell the land for anything. "Anything that's strong enough," Bill Sutton said one day when we were talking about it.

Or so the Suttons, being Northerners, thought.

But Aunt Charlotte didn't die. She flourished. As she flourished something seemed to dry up in Daniel Sutton. It became a question if Aunt Charlotte wasn't the better man, and if she wouldn't in fact outlast the whole Sutton tribe.

"Do you know, Martha," said Thorn abruptly, "I don't know just what's happened to Uncle Dan. About Aunt Charlotte, I mean."

"How?"

"Well, all things being equal there's no reason why she shouldn't stay in the cabin. Heaven knows she doesn't hurt anybody. She's picturesque and when we've got people to entertain she's a godsend with her rabbit's foot and love-potions and sticks for chasing devils. And Uncle likes her too. But she won't *sell*. She owns that spot of ground and Uncle can't get it. I swear, Martha, it's killing him."

"Perfect rot, Thorn," I said. "You're as bad as Lillie. Last Friday when it was thundering and raining and we had all that lightning, she insisted Aunt Charlotte had conjured Mr. Sutton and he was goin' to die hisself right in his tracks."

Thorn brushed her hair violently away from her forehead.

"I almost believe it, Martha."

Her distress was so genuine that I was a little alarmed.

"Don't be an idiot," I protested. "Ask Professor Sykes what's wrong. He'll tell you your uncle's got a complex, or a fixation or something. He's set his heart on having the whole piece of land and he won't be happy until he gets it. No one's ever stood out against him in all his life, at least for long, and here's the old colored woman who was a slave almost forty years, who can neither read nor write, but who simply won't sell her land. It's very simple. It's sort of a frustration business. I don't know exactly what it is but it seems it's what people get when they can't have what they want and there's nobody to spank them soundly and send them to bed."

"Call it what you please," Thorn replied wearily. "I agree

15

with Lillie. Aunt Charlotte's conjured him and he's goin' to die. What's it matter how she's done it? All conjuring demands a psychological victim. Uncle Dan's a perfect one."

She was deadly serious, lying there with eyes closed, traces of tears for Franklin Knox still on her smooth pale ivory cheeks. I got up uncomfortably and moved to the window. I was thinking of Lillie's old black face and her skinny bony hands pointing through our kitchen window to the lightning over Seaton Hall: "Aunt Charlotte's conjured him. He'll die hisself in his tracks some night."

I hardly noticed the banks of white and pink magnolia blossoms until one large petal fell from a bloom and fluttered down against the black-green ground of the box hedge. Involuntarily my eye followed it until it came to rest in a yellow-gloved hand stretched out to catch it. I looked at the hand and then at the man standing in the drive, looking up at the magnolia tree. It was my friend in grey flannels whom I'd left sitting on my garden wall. He saw me, and raised his hat and bowed. I heard Lafayette open the great mahogany door to admit him.

As I turned back to Thorn I had a distinct feeling of impending diaster.

III

Ordinarily when I have alarming forebodings about anything I go out to the club and play nine holes of golf. Surely nothing can ever be as bad as the average woman who hasn't any hard physical work to do can make it by spending a couple of solitary hours thinking about it.

As a matter of fact if Thorn, who's normally so irresistibly level-headed and gaily matter-of-fact, hadn't been so upset about her uncle, I think the presence of a handsome dark-skinned young man in the court below would never have occurred to me as the least bit strange. What was more natural, when you got down to it, than that the man, having asked if this was the Sutton place, should turn up at it a little later? And that he should choose to pause a moment and catch a drifting magnolia petal in his yellow-gloved hand was hardly sinister.

Nevertheless when I went back across the room and sat down at the end of the sofa, I was distinctly uneasy. Thorn was occupied in repairing the damage her tears had done and in pushing her curly hair into more formal waves with slim dexterous fingers. For myself I felt exactly as I do when I've been driving on a glaring sunny day wearing dark glasses. I gradually forget that it's really brilliantly clear with the sky blue, and find myself driving faster and faster to escape the terrifying brazen sulphur sky and ominously darkened fields.

I don't know whether it's odd or not that my foreboding was so completely justified.

Of course I'd known the rumor in the town that Mr. Sutton had become unreasonably concerned with the business of Aunt Charlotte's land. Only the night before Dr. Knox had said it was preying on the old gentleman's mind. Miss Alice Marks, a decayed gentlewoman of the old school, had remarked when we met that morning in the local Piggly Wiggly over the basket of fresh lima beans that it seemed curious to her that having so much as Mr. Daniel Sutton had he should be so determined to get Aunt Charlotte's plot. She knew nothing about it, of course, except what she'd heard from one of her guests (Miss Marks ran a genteel boarding-house), but it seemed most strange that a man of so much prominence should be so small. Her butler had told her that Mr. Sutton had offered twenty-five thousand for the land. It seemed a great deal for thirty feet of land, didn't I think so?

I quite truthfully said I did think so—knowing the care with which Mr. Sutton usually spent money. I still under-estimated Daniel Sutton's passion not to be thwarted.

Archie McNab, the superintendent of the college build-ings and grounds, said it sure made him laugh the way the old boy was hipped on getting the old lady's dump and he didn't mean maybe. It was his opinion that the old bird was as crazy as a bed-bug.

I think that is a fair cross-section of local white opinion. Colored opinion was fairly expressed by my Lillie: "That ol' devil goin' get Aunt Charlotte's place if he busts hisself."

That was apparently the conclusion his family had come to. The manner of his busting hisself seemed the only thing left to decide.

As I've known the Suttons intimately since they've been in Landover, I've never felt the necessity of telling them the continuous gossip about them that goes the rounds. They hear enough of it without the help of their friends.

Thorn went back abruptly after a long silence. "I won't marry Franklin, Martha, if Uncle Dan cuts me out of his will. I told Franklin so last night."

I looked at her, rather surprised at the finality in her voice.

17

She was sitting with chin cupped in her hands, her elbows on her knees, her jaw set tightly. I had less doubt than ever that she was a Sutton.

"If money's that important, my dear," I began, a little sententiously, I'm afraid, "I think you're very wise."

"It isn't that. Although you know how beastly important it is as well as I do," she went on warmly. "Two people can't possibly be happy or get anything out of life, or give anything to each other, without it. And you know it."

I saw myself forced into the very unwelcome role of defending small incomes.

"That's true up to a point," I said. "But it doesn't mean that you have to have a million dollars for you and Franklin to get on. After all, he makes a fairly decent income, doesn't he? It's certainly above the average; and eventually he'll do very well. What did he say when you told him what you'd decided?"

She flushed painfully.

"He said maybe I was right, and that it wasn't fair for him to ask me to marry him because he'd never have the money Uncle has. Said he never wanted it. That if I thought it was important, and couldn't get used to living on a simpler scale he'd release me."

She stared straight ahead of her. The corners of her mouth quivered dangerously.

"Oh," I said callously. "What did you say?"

"I said that if that was all he cared about me, it was just as well I knew it too. Then I came inside. I haven't seen him since."

"Are you surprised?" I asked. "After all, Thorn, it isn't quite as if he were a grocery clerk at seven dollars a week. It's no particular virtue of yours that you're Daniel Sutton's niece. You couldn't help it. On the other hand Franklin is what he is and what he's going to be entirely by his own intelligence and jolly hard work."

"I know that."

"But don't you see the position you put him in? He can't say money doesn't matter. All he can do is one of two things. He can go back to Baltimore and work like poison to make enough money to marry you. That takes time and he can't be sure you'll not up and marry young Fairweather, since it's money you've got to have. Or he can tell you to go to blazes, you're not worth what he's got to offer you."

She didn't move a muscle. She sat with her chin still in her cupped hands, staring sullenly in front of her. Her face was a mixture of shadowy moving passions that I'd never thought

18

of her as having. The grim tight mouth, the set jaw and flat smoldering eyes were new phases of Thorn Carter to me.

She got up suddenly and began to pace the room.

"There's no use saying I don't care, Martha," she said huskily after a little. "I do care. I'll marry Franklin, if he'll have me after last night. He'll probably think I'm just a mercenary pig. But it's not fair of Uncle Dan and I'll get even with him. You'll see."

Her voice rose passionately. Just then there was a tap at the door. Thorn stopped quickly.

"Come in," she said. "Oh hello, Dan."

Thorn's two cousins, Mr. Sutton's sons, came in. Dan sank down on the sofa beside me.

"Hello, Martha," he said. "Cigarettes somewhere, Thorn? Anything'll do. Thanks."

Bill Sutton stopped wandering around the room. He's two years younger than Dan and rather quicker.

"What's the matter with you, Thorn?" he said.

"Nothing."

"That's the trouble with most of us," Bill said philosophically. "What's the matter with you, Martha? How's the good old endowment fund?"

"Rotten, thanks," I said.

"Heard the latest, Thorn, about the station?"

"No. Something new?"

"Somebody's trying to stick the old man for twenty-five thousand."

"I heard that. Who is it, do you know?"

"Nope. A lawyer called up this morning. I guess we'll know by night."

"Why the devil he doesn't let them have the place and be blowed I can't see," Dan remarked. "Is this an ashtray?"

Thorn rescued a bit of old Venetian glass.

"No. Here, use this."

Dan looked sorrowfully at the half-pint pewter mug handed to him.

"Women," he said, "have no feeling for these things. This is for beer. Not ashes."

"I don't see," said Thorn, "why anybody would want a service station there."

"It's all bluff, if you ask me," Bill said, filling his pipe. "Somebody's got hold of it, and he's going to make Dad pay through the nose. Everybody knows he's crazy about it."

We were interrupted by the precipitate entrance of Susan Atwood, Miss Mildred Carter's nineteen-year-old ward. Susan always entered precipitately.

"Hello everybody." She pitched a floppy tan straw hat to the other side of the room and collapsed in a deep chair.

"My dears! There's the most ravaging creature down stairs you've *ever* seen! Thorn, he's marvellous! He uses too much lipstick though, they're sort of sticky red."

"Susan, how *awful!"*

"Not at all! Au contraire! He's marvellous, he's *wonderful!* And what's he doing here? No one asks? I'll tell you anyway. He was asking Matthew if he could see Uncle Dan. I was coming out of the library."

"Susan!" said Dan with concern. "You weren't reading a book?"

"No; I'd left my racket there. And Miss Atwood said to the charming stranger, 'If you're not in a hurry you'd better come back Friday, Uncle is not in a receptive mood.' "

Thorn stared at her.

"Wait till Matthew tells Uncle Dan that."

"Not necessary, my pet. At precisely that moment Uncle Dan appears at the front door. I sha'n't lie to you, I wasn't very happy. But I said, pleasantly and with great calm, 'Uncle Dan, I've just told this gentleman who's just arrived from Spain that you will be delighted to buy whatever he's got.' With that I left."

"What did Uncle Dan say?"

"My dear, I said I *left.* I closed my eyes and my ears and I went. And as I came up the stairs I could feel the fiery breath on the back of my neck."

Bill smiled patiently.

"What *is* the distinguished foreign gentleman doing, by the way?"

"He's staying to lunch, for one thing. I listened from the landing."

"You'd better stay too, then, Martha," Thorn said dryly. "If you don't there'll be a murder. Millionaire slays impulsive nineteen-year-old."

"Surely, Martha. If only to see what the beautiful man sold Uncle Dan."

I shook my head.

"I've got to get home."

"That's silly," Susan answered calmly. "Anyway, you can't. I just met Mrs. Hopper and Mrs. Joyce coming out of your place seven minutes ago, and I told them you were going to be here for lunch and play golf with me in the afternoon. So that's settled. Oh, and I met Miss Eliza Baker too, this morning, and she stopped me and said she was *so* sorry to hear

20

that Aunt Charlotte had sold her land to some oil company for a service station."

Here Susan made a long and doleful face so exactly like Miss Eliza's that even Bill had to smile.

"What did you say?"

"I didn't say a thing."

"I'll bet," said Dan.

"Or not much. I just said Yes, it was such a lousy place the way it is, and Uncle Dan thought a nice scarlet station would be a convenient landmark for Bill when he gets home in his usual condition at three in the morning."

"Oh shut up," Bill said.

I wish I had been clairvoyant that morning. Maybe I could have recognized then that there were already well in motion the three currents of event, one of which—so everyone thought later—was leading us swiftly and inevitably to the murder of Daniel Sutton. There was the situation of Thorn Carter and Franklin Knox; there was the rising complication of Aunt Charlotte's thirty feet of land; and there were the strange happenings connected with the brilliant-eyed, faultlessly dressed stranger.

IV

I stayed to lunch. Looking back on the events of these few days beginning with the arrival of the stranger, they seem to me almost like a play in which I was a spectator who'd got mixed up, in some way, with the actors on the stage. My talk with Thorn was a prologue. This lunch was an opening scene that moved slowly, putting everything in its place so that the rest of the incredible business must inevitably follow. And I think I must have got in everybody's way very much, as a spectator would who left his seat and started wandering about on the stage, talking to Hamlet, say, so that he hadn't time to see his father's ghost, or pick up poor Yorick's skull as the grave-digger tossed it up.

For some reason Daniel Sutton came to the table in—for him—a fairly genial mood. He was one of those men whose family and servants wait for his arrival with a vague anticipatory dread, never knowing quite what to expect by way of atmosphere. Sometimes Mr. Sutton was, as Thorn always put it, on a rampage. Sometimes he was sunk in an ominous sullen silence; at others, such as to-day, he was moderately genial.

Mr. Sutton was never, except to a very few people, of whom I was one and Dr. Knox another, what you might call gracious or even pleasant. He was indomitably stubborn and selfish. His high voice had an unpleasant sneering quality; so did his thin smooth-shaven upper lip. Pale grey eyes glinted at you myopically through thick rimless lenses under a pair of beetling black brows. He had a habit of running his fat hands through his dry sparse grey hair so that it crackled brittlely. He smoked cigars, continuously and savagely, but he seldom drank, and then only a little light wine from his pre-Volstead cellar in New York. His two sons, Thorn Carter his niece, and Wally Fenton, a nephew, were without a doubt afraid of him. At least they avoided being around him when they could, or ever taking issue with him. There's no doubt they had considerable respect for his achievements in the industrial world, and even a sort of timid affection for him. Susan Atwood, I think—except of course Miss Mildred Carter, his dead wife's sister—was the only person in the house, servants included, who didn't leave when he appeared if possible. Susan was herself on all occasions. Neither Mr. Sutton nor anyone else had been known to dampen her in the least.

When we came down Mr. Sutton presented Sebastien Baca.

Mr. Baca was, it turned out, a Mexican, apparently of considerable wealth, whose ancestors, we were told, had stood on the cliffs with Balboa when he first sighted the waters of the Pacific.

Susan was entranced. Bill asserted in a whisper his belief that she had only a vague idea what the waters of the Pacific were, and was undoubtedly confusing Balboa and Columbus. I thought Susan could certainly hear these comments, but if so they had no effect on the quality of her admiring attention.

"I've got to hand it to him," Bill said in an undertone. "He's the only person she's ever listened to ten seconds without breaking in to ask what time it is, or if it rained last night."

Sebastien Baca was interesting. He told us about the life on the great ranchos of Mexico and New Mexico. He spoke careful, beautiful English, and was considerably more cultivated than the two Suttons or their cousin Wally Fenton, who was there.

"It's a beautiful country," he said, smiling first at Miss Carter, Daniel Sutton's sister-in-law, and then at Susan. "My people once owned the great ranch that you now own, Mr.

22

Sutton. El Rancho del Ojo del Espiritu Santo. The Ranch of the Spring of the Holy Ghost."

"What a gorgeous name! Uncle Dan, do you really own a ranch named that?"

"The Spaniards were a poetic people, and a religious people," remarked the Mexican, smiling again at her enthusiasm. "And the country is so beautiful one is never surprised. The sun rising behind the Sierras, the rosy dawn in the mountains, and in the evening the amethyst shadows deepening in the valleys to the bluest ultramarine—it is so lovely! At night the stars are like golden bees on a velvet ground. The mountains, the desert." He shrugged his shoulders as if deprecating his own enthusiasm. "They are sublime!"

He went on to tell us about his own people, and the library in the mission monastery built by their padres. He told us about the Spanish treasure supposed to be buried in the hills, in caves whose mouths had long ago been concealed by quick-growing mesquite. One story that I liked particularly he told us about an ancestor of his with Balboa who had wearied of carrying his share of the treasure taken from a native settlement. He offered it to a friend, who refused it. Then he threw it—thousands of dollars in pearls and beaten gold—over his shoulder. There it still lies, somewhere in the sand. His grandfather had told him the story.

"I met your grandfather once," said Daniel Sutton.

"My grandfather was bitterly opposed to selling the ranch," returned Sebastien Baca simply. "So was my father, who was a young man then. But younger brothers have no importance in my family."

He shrugged his elegant shoulders with good-humored resignation, and smiled engagingly at Miss Carter.

By this time he had completely captivated her. His undeniable charm, his quick changes of mood, from a deprecatory regret at the passing of the old patriarchal order to a warm enthusiasm about his country, and from cultivated suaveness to an almost child-like naïveté, were delightful. At first Bill and Dan exchanged mildly derisive glances, especially over Susan's wide-eyed and very flattering eagerness. They gave it up in a few minutes, and listened to Mr. Baca with quite evident interest.

Wallace Fenton was the only person at the table who had an air of completely uninterested boredom. To look at him sitting across the table next to Susan one got the impression that if that person didn't stop talking he for one would find it utterly impossible to take food. None of us like Wally very much, I'm afraid. He's Mr. Sutton's nephew and spends as

23

much time at Seaton Hall as he can manage. I don't suppose his cousins are actually rude to him, but there's certainly none of that fine camaraderie that exists between the four of them.

"What's the matter with the golden-haired boy?" whispered Bill sotto voce to me as his cousin stifled a yawn and lighted a cigarette.

"Doesn't like Mexico," I replied.

Wally's hair is as black, and almost as shinily lacquered in appearance, as that of the Mexican now at the end of the table. His eyes are dark, although he is usually referred to as the blue-eyed boy. If such designations bother him at all no one has ever noticed it. In fact when at Seaton Hall he practically ignores everybody except his uncle and Susan.

Bill grinned.

"He's probably returning thanks that he didn't take the Holy Ghost ranch when Dad offered it to him last year. Picture him going in for the purple sunsets and the lone coyote?"

His cousin heard him and twisted his lips into a bored and not unfriendly half-smile that managed to tilt his tiny, perfect black mustache to a very devilish angle. He raised his brows and slowly blew a thin wand of smoke towards the ceiling.

Daniel Sutton, who pretends to a certain convenient deafness but always manages to hear anything said in a whisper, glanced sharply at Bill and then at his nephew. I think he was going to make some remark when Lafayette entered the dining room with a telegram on his little silver tray.

"It's fo' Mistah Wally, ma'am," the old darkey said.

"May I, Aunt Mildred?"

He tore open the yellow envelope. Although I'd hesitate to say that any of us were staring at him, I don't think any of us missed the slight contraction of his dark features, or the tiny smile of satisfaction that followed. At any rate I didn't.

"It's from Arbuthnot-Howe, Aunt. You remember, Uncle Dan, he was in New York last winter and I brought him around?"

"Is he the Englishman? Hasn't he got a title or something?" Susan asked hopefully.

"He will have when his uncle, brother and two nephews die," Wally replied. "He's too old for you anyway, Sue. Furthermore, he got shot up in the war and has a game leg."

"Oh," said Susan.

I can't ever remember that these youngsters of Susan's age

24

were almost infants in arms in 1914 to 1918. The thought always comes as a new shock to me.

"He's in Washington, Aunt Mildred. Could we have him over for the week-end?"

"Surely," Miss Carter smiled. "And Mr. Baca is staying too—aren't you?"

I think everybody had forgotten Mr. Baca. That is, everybody but me. Of course I wasn't as much interested in Arbuthnot-Howe as they were, and I was interested in Mr. Baca. When Wally mentioned the name of his British friend I had been looking at the portrait of Thorn Carter's grandfather over the mantel just above his head. My glance in getting back to the table quite accidentally dropped to Mr. Baca on its way, and there it rested for a second just as Wally said "Arbuthnot-Howe." I don't know exactly what the emotion in Baca's face was, it was so instantaneously gone; but I do know this: Sebastien Baca was perfectly familiar with that name. What's more, it meant a lot to him. I didn't of course know in what way, but I knew that Sebastien Baca would have preferred not to see Mr. Arbuthnot-Howe.

And just at that moment he said, "I shall be delighted, madam. It's so kind of you." He bowed and offered his arm to Miss Carter as we left the dining room.

"I'll drive over, I guess, and pick him up," Wally said. "Want to go, Sue?"

"Not if he's got a game leg, I don't," Susan returned callously.

"Okay," said Wally.

V

After lunch we all went out on the wide verandah that Mr. Sutton built across the back of the house, looking down the long green vista of formal tree-lined garden into the grey-blue haze of Seaton River. Mr. Sutton sat down by me and cocked an angry pale grey eye at me.

"Heard the latest?" he demanded with a sardonic chuckle.

"No. What?" I replied.

"They're buying that old woman's property for a service station."

"Well, that's simple," I said. "All you have to do is get an injunction against it. I was afraid when I heard somebody was buying it—I *had* heard about that—they'd really be offensive."

25

He snorted violently, bit his strong yellow teeth into a cigar and spat the end out with more feeling than I like to see.

"Damn scoundrels," he muttered savagely.

"Who's behind it?" I asked tentatively, holding a match for him.

He puffed silently a moment. His face developed a curiously mottled look that was positively alarming.

"I don't know who's behind it, Martha," he said. "But I'm going to find out. When I do somebody's going to sweat . . . plenty."

He breathed heavily and his thick nostrils quivered. I began to understand Thorn's distress. He certainly wasn't normal on the subject.

"Do you know Reverdy Hawkins?" he demanded suddenly. "You seem to enjoy a wide acquaintance in the town."

People usually regard his expression when he makes jokes of that sort as a sneer, but I don't think he meant it as such.

"Yes," I said. "He's a lawyer. Aunt Charlotte's nephew. I used to have a cook with an epileptic son. Reverdy got him out of jail once a week for stealing, at three dollars a throw. I finally persuaded Anna May it would be better to put the boy in Crownsville."

Mr. Sutton mumbled a rounder oath than was polite.

"Reverdy is honest as far as he goes," I went on. "Also, if there's an idea involved in what he's doing, you can be sure it's not his idea. Somebody's putting him up to it. Probbly somebody white."

Here we were characteristically interrupted by Susan.

"Martha, if we're going to play golf we'd better be getting on with it."

She perched on the arm of Mr. Sutton's chair and put her hands over his mouth as he was about to speak.

"Anyway, Uncle Dan's not allowed to talk about Aunt Charlotte after meals. Bad for his digestion, bad for everybody else's."

I think I almost expected to see Susan's small brown hands bitten off at the wrists and bleeding stumps waving about. Mr. Sutton however took it with surprising grace.

"Promise, Uncle Dan!" she demanded loudly in his right ear, still keeping her hands firmly over his mouth. "Yes or no?"

He tried, not very hard, to free himself, and finally nodded. Susan let him go. I breathed much more easily.

"All right. I'm ready," I said.

"We'll be at the house for you in half an hour," Susan finished up. She manages everything for everybody—giving or saving no end of trouble, whichever way you look at it.

"By the way, Martha," Mr. Sutton said as I was going inside. "If you happen to see J. K., tell him I'd like to see him."

I nodded. J. K. is Dr. Knox, the president of Landover College and Mr. Sutton's only intimate friend.

It wasn't in the least odd that I did see Dr. Knox just as I crossed Duke of Gloucester Street. Landover is so small that you see almost everyone you know almost every day, unless they're sick or out of town. Dr. Knox was on his way to our house.

"Hello, Martha," he smiled. I smiled too, because he has an infectious twinkle in his shrewd blue eyes. Even if you don't quite know what the joke is, or perhaps suspect it's on you, you nevertheless have to smile too.

"Hello!" I said.

"I was just going in to see your husband about young Baker. I'm told he's flunking Anthropology and won't be eligible for the Williams game."

"How awful!" I said. "I hope you'll think of my helpless infants, and our poor cat with five kittens born this very morning, and not throw him to the alumni."

Dr. Knox gave his charming subterranean chuckle.

"You never take these things seriously enough, Martha."

"It's you, sir," I retorted. "You don't realize that if it weren't for athletics such harmony would prevail that American colleges would peacefully go to sleep like Oxford and Cambridge. As a matter of fact, I think the coach said he didn't really need young Baker. That's why Ben's flunking him, of course. I suspect that, anyway, because the other night the coach and Ben were having a highball in Ben's study and later Ben told me he'd at last persuaded him that Bob Lacey was the better goalkeeper of the two."

Dr. Knox smiled quietly. Then his face sobered quickly.

"As a matter of fact it was you I wanted to see, Martha," he said as we went up on the porch. "Let's sit out here."

"What is it, J. K.?" I asked in alarm, his manner was so grave.

"Have you seen Thorn Carter this morning?"

I nodded.

"What did she say?"

"She said she intended to marry Franklin if he'd have her. She was frightfully upset. I hope Franklin will call her up or something."

Dr. Knox shook his grand white head.

"I'm afraid he won't, Martha."

27

"Where is he?"

"He went to Baltimore this morning. He's very deeply hurt, I'm afraid."

"Oh, it's absurd!" I scoffed. "If he can't overlook Thorn's outbursts—heaven knows they're rare enough—then he can't be very much in love with her."

"You're overlooking his own pride, my dear."

"Oh, my dear sir!" I said. I was getting a little fed up with the business of Thorn and Franklin Knox. "They make me . . . Well, you send Franklin to me and I'll give him a piece of my mind."

Just then my impractical professor of Anthropology appeared in the door.

"Always giving away something she hasn't got—aren't you? How are you, sir?"

Dr. Knox smiled.

"All right, Martha, I'll send him around. See what you can do. I'd like to see it patched up. I think they're a good match."

"Oh, Mr. Sutton told me to tell you he'd like to see you, J. K.," I said. "And look—there comes Reverdy Hawkins. He's on his way to see Mr. Sutton now. I wouldn't like to be in his shoes."

I pointed up the road to the absurd figure of the colored lawyer with his brown derby and frock coat above a pair of grey flannels that we'd bought for Ben in Regent Street the last time we were in London. He wore enormous horn-rimmed spectacles and carried a brief case and looked very important indeed.

He came opposite the porch and seeing us swept off his hat in an elaborate salutation that was an irresistibly funny caricature of Dr. Knox's fine Southern manner. I caught Dr. Knox's eye and we both laughed, and Reverdy Hawkins laughed too, though one could see from his face that he didn't think anything was very funny.

He opened the gate and came to the bottom step.

"Good evenin', Doctor. Evenin', Miss. Mighty warm day, sir."

It wasn't particularly warm, as a matter of fact, but I could quite understand Reverdy's thinking it was.

"How's John Thomas getting on?" I asked.

"Tolable, tolable. Right smart of business comin' in, but things pretty slow jest now."

John Thomas was Reverdy's son who'd just opened a catering establishment. The general feeling was that he was bootlegging; it was an assumption based solely on his new

Chrysler. In Landover people don't get new cars by serving mint-flavored ice tea and cakes with pink frosting at garden parties.

I felt rather sorry for Reverdy, mopping his glistening mahogany dome with a green silk handkerchief. He didn't want to stay and talk to us, but he wanted to put off facing Daniel Sutton in his den as long as he could. Obviously a victim of his own guile.

Wally drove by just then in his blue sports Packard and waved at us.

"Hawkins!" he called out. "Mr. Sutton's expecting you. Better move along!"

"Yassuh!" he said, although Wally was already half-way down the road.

Reverdy stretched his long black neck, pulled at his limp wing collar and adjusted the great red glass pin in his orange and black striped knit tie.

"Ah reckons Ah'd better be goin' on. Ah wouldn' want to keep Mistah Sutton waitin'."

"Good day, Reverdy," said Dr. Knox.

The amused smile on his face faded with Reveredy's reluctant figure. He turned to me.

"What's this all about, Martha?"

"Aunt Charlotte. I don't know exactly what it is, but Mr. Sutton's furious. She's finally sold the place, or decided to. Whoever it is is threatening to put up a service station."

Dr. Knox said nothing for a moment.

"What's behind it?" he asked at last.

"I don't know—except twenty-five thousand dollars. At least that's the sum the townspeople have got hold of. Do you think Mr. Sutton would pay that much to keep a service station off the spot?"

Dr. Knox was silent again.

"Yes," he said slowly. "I think he would. In his present mood he would pay anything. He said last week he'd get that ground, and get Charlotte off it, if it took the rest of his life and every cent he had to do it."

I looked at him incredulously. His face was grave.

"Who heard him say that, J. K.?" I asked. It seemed to me that I was beginning to see into this business.

He looked at me quickly.

"It was after dinner one night last week," he replied. "I was there, Bill and Dan, and Franklin. That's all."

"Wasn't Thorn there?"

"Oh yes. Yes, she came in while we were talking."

VI

I didn't go out with Thorn and the others to play golf that afternoon. An important point had come up as to whether the Faculty Wives' Club should give a tea-dance during Commencement or confine their efforts to entertaining parents and friends of the graduating class at a garden party. Personally I was for the garden party. Nothing makes me feel my thirty-odd years more than undergraduates and their girls at tea-dances. I suppose it's chiefly because quite unconsciously they regard you as tottering most definitely on the brink. When I go back to my college homecoming all my professors seem years younger to me than they did while I was a student. How much greater the gulf is between twenty and thirty than between thirty and forty!

Anyway, I went to the meeting to vote against a tea-dance. On my way home I remembered I hadn't got Aunt Charlotte the unbleached muslin I promised her the week before and stopped in at The Ladies' Store to get it. I was coming out with my parcel under my arm when I met Mr. Sullivan, Landover's prosecuting attorney, just coming up from Court House Square.

"How are you, Mrs. Niles?"

"I'm well, how are you?"

"Tolerable, thanks."

"Mr. Sullivan, you sound just like Reverdy Hawkins."

He grinned.

"Glad I don't feel like him. He was just in to see me. He's a scared boy."

"What's he trying to do?" I asked guilelessly.

"I don't exactly know. Seems to have something up his sleeve. He wanted to know what the legal definition of conspiracy was. I guess he wanted to know how far he could go without Sutton's getting him on a criminal charge."

"Did you tell him?"

"I told him if he was wise he'd let Sutton alone. I told him he had as much chance as a jack-rabbit if Sutton gets Nathan Rand down here on him."

Mr. Rand is Mr. Sutton's New York lawyer, who happens also to be an alumnus of Landover College, and furthermore one of its Visitors and Governors. I mention all this because, as it happens, he played a small but very important part in the terrible event that was coming so rapidly on us.

"But there's one thing Sutton and Rand and the whole blessed kit and caboodle of 'em can't do," Mr. Sullivan added, with another grin. "They can't make old Charlotte sell to 'em, and they can't stop her selling to her nephew Reverdy if she wants to. And they can't stop him selling to anybody he pleases."

I caught the shrewd twinkle of his blue Irish eyes.

"So that's it," I said. "She's selling to Reverdy."

"I don't know it officially. But that's what my wife tells me. And she gets more hot tips than any state police you've ever seen. I've often thought of putting her on the pay-roll. Wouldn't quite do, would it?"

We parted at Mr. Sullivan's gate on York Road a few doors above me, and I went on down the street to give Aunt Charlotte my parcel—and, I suspect, to hear whatever I could.

I opened the rickety gate and crossed the little patch of garden that divided her whitewashed cabin from York Road. The door was open. When I looked in I think I got one of the worst shocks of my life. There was a dingy little parlor hung with heavy gilt-framed crayon enlargements of the biggest lot of forebears you ever saw; and Daniel Sutton was sitting on the horsehair sofa at the end of the room.

Aunt Charlotte was in her chair near the door. When she saw me she got up painfully. She's pretty much crippled with rheumatism.

"Law, Miss Marty, is that you honey? You ain' been see me for days."

She hobbled along on her heavy stick to meet me.

"Sit down, Aunt Charlotte. How's your rheumatism?"

"Mighty poorly, honey. Mah laig ain' much 'count. If Ah could Ah'd sell it for a yaller dawg an' shoot him."

She wagged her old head that was like an ancient withered gourd except for two shrewd bright eyes and four small patches of neatly braided white wool on top of it.

"I'se poorly, honey. The doctor's here yes'day, an' he tells me Ah got move away from this'yere water. It's done got lime in it. Lime ain' good for some folks, they jus' nach'lly cain' stand it."

I glanced involuntarily at Mr. Sutton, sitting cross-legged on the old sofa, listening to all this without a word. His face was expressionless, which was an unusual thing.

"It's been mighty good for you, Aunt Charlotte," I said.

31

"Not many people live to be ninety-nine and stay as young as you are."

"Deed Ah ain' so young, honey."

Mr. Sutton spoke abruptly. "Where are you going to go, Charlotte?"

"Deed an' Ah' don' know, sir. They say they's a place whe' it ain' never col', and whe' they ain' no lime in the water, whe' they can take me to. I don' want no other winter like las' one."

"You be careful, Charlotte," Mr. Sutton said with more humanity than I'd heard him use toward the old woman, "that those fellows don't put you down there at Shepherd's Hill."

For an instant stark primitive fear appeared in the old woman's eyes. She gave a sudden start and clutched at her stick. It was the one constant fear of her life that somebody would put her in the colored old people's home. In fact—as I that minute remembered—her dislike of Daniel Sutton rose from precisely that fear. When he first came to Landover he suggested that in all faith she'd be more comfortable there.

Now she looked dumbly first at him, then at me.

"They won' do that, Miss Marty," she mumbled. But I saw she wasn't confident of it.

Mr. Sutton got up abruptly.

"Are you going back, Martha?"

I nodded, but caught the dumb appeal in poor old Charlotte's eyes.

"I'll be back later," I told her. "Would you like some rice pudding for supper?"

She rocked back and forth. I didn't really want to leave her.

When we had gone Mr. Sutton said, "That'll give her something to think about."

"It was rather cruel, don't you think?"

"Nonsense. I don't know—quite—who's behind all this business, but it's nobody who's going to give a continental about what Charlotte wants or doesn't want."

"Mr. Sullivan says Reverdy is buying the place."

Mr. Sutton snorted derisively.

"That damned blockhead doesn't know what he's doing. I grilled him for twenty minutes. I couldn't exactly get out of him who's hired him. But I've got a pretty good guess, Martha."

He gave me a look so black with vexation, bitterness and sheer wrath that I almost shuddered.

"Who is it?" I said, as evenly as I could.

He was silent. I thought for a moment that I'd been unduly inquisitive, although I really knew that he wanted to tell it to somebody. I glanced at him. He was walking with his hands clasped behind his back, jaw set like a steel trap. Suddenly he looked coldly at me.

"It's someone in my own family, Martha," he said.

I looked away.

"That's what you thought too?" he asked quickly.

"Oh no!"

"Then you're as big a fool as I was. But I don't believe you."

We were nearing the gate.

"I don't have to tell you that this is between the two of us," he said. I nodded.

We reached the gate. I was going on when Wally Fenton drove up complete with friend, a perfectly gigantic man with a high bronzed forehead and blondish hair.

Wally drew up and introduced us.

"How d'you do?" he said.

His voice was very deep and very English, naturally. I still remember that moment, as well—or almost as well—as when I first saw Mr. Sebastien Baca. And in his way the Englishman was as perfect as the Southerner. I don't think I've met many people as irresistibly charming at first sight as Colonel Arbuthnot-Howe. He had a fine strong face, rugged and kindly, and steely amused blue eyes. We shook hands and his were enormous cordial brown paws.

We talked a few moments. Mr. Sutton remembered him and was disposed to be quite friendly, rather to Wally's relief, I thought.

After a bit they drove on into the grounds, and I continued homeward along York Road. Once I turned around. Mr. Sutton was slowly making his way, head down, hands clasped behind him, across the campus. He was walking very slowly. I guessed he was on his way to the Knox house on College Green. I had a cold sick feeling inside of me.

VII

When I got back to the house I found a message from Miss Carter asking us over to the dinner. I was still considerably disturbed by the events of the last half hour. But by the time

33

I'd arbitrated in the nursery dessert question, compromised on Peter Rabbit, found my husband's studs, dressed myself and tied my husband's tie the Sutton business had faded to insignificance. I did remember when we set out to take Aunt Charlotte her rice pudding.

She was sitting on her front stoop, wagging her head in dismal monotony.

"Evenin' Mr. Ben," she said dully. "Miss Marty, does you s'spose that worthless Reve'dy'd play me tricks?"

"I don't know, Aunt Charlotte."

"Don' you sit, honey, you spoil that frock. It's mighty purty an' you powerful careless."

I sat down anyway.

"Now look, Aunt Charlotte," I said. "I know this. That business about lime in the water is silly rot."

She shook her head. Like millions of her betters she was impressed by plausible quackery.

"How much is Reverdy paying you, Aunt Charlotte?"

She hesitated only a second. "Ten thousand dollars." She said it dreamily, almost chanting it.

While I was thinking that over the college bell struck seven.

"I've got to go, Aunt Charlotte. But I want you to promise me this: that you won't do anything until you let us know. You haven't signed anything, have you?"

"No'ndeed, I ain' sign nothin'," she replied stoutly.

"Then don't before I see you again. Promise!"

She mumbled an incoherent something.

"Promise, Aunt Charlotte!"

"Yas'm. Ah promises."

——Not that I expected it would do much good.

Everyone was in the drawing room when we arrived except Mr. Sutton and the gentleman from Mexico.

We spoke to Miss Carter and Susan drew me to a sofa beside her.

"Martha, have you met Colonel Arbuthnot-Howe?"

Both of us nodded.

"He's wonderful, he knows all about elephant hunting in Africa. 'Tracking was difficult in the extreme. As there was a total absence of rain, it was impossible to distinguish the spoor of two days' date . . .'"

"Shut up," said Bill from across the room. "The trouble with Susan," he explained to Colonel Arbuthnot-Howe, "is that her Fifth Reader made such an impression on her that she's never forgot it, and never opened a book since."

"That's a lie. I read the *Sheik.* That was years ago. Say, where's Uncle Dan?"

She got up hastily and I gathered set out to look for him. As she went out Bill grinned broadly at her.

"It's not so," she said, tossing her head impudently. "*Is he* going to stay, Auntie?"

Miss Carter nodded. "He's a very interesting and well-bred young man," she said gently.

"Have you met Mr. Baca?" I asked Colonel Arbuthnot-Howe. Rather by way of conversation than anything else. Then I remembered something.

"I think not," he said pleasantly. "Although I might have, you know. I've met a great many people."

"He knows you."

"Really? What makes you think so?"

"Nothing really. Just that this noon at lunch when your name was mentioned he looked for a second as though . . . well, as though he knew you. It may have been my imagination."

He shrugged his shoulders.

"Is this he?"

"Yes."

Susan came back followed by her uncle and Mr. Baca.

"Look, I found them. Playing geography—had a map pinned on the wall," she announced. "You two haven't met," she went on, turning to Mr. Baca and Colonel Arbuthnot-Howe. "You'd better, you have to share the same bathroom."

The two men bowed with splendid formality. Miss Carter looked mildly pained and infinitely resigned. Clearly she had given up hope of Susan.

Lafayette brought in cocktails and Mr. Baca drifted over to talk to Miss Carter. Susan perched on the arm of her aunt's chair. Mr. Sutton was talking to Arbuthnot-Howe, and Thorn, Bill, Dan and I were looking at the sporting pages of a Baltimore paper trying to find out how much we'd lost on Tiger Cat in the second race.

Quite by chance I glanced up and caught Colonel Arbuthnot-Howe's eye. He smiled and shook his head. He *didn't* know Sebastien Baca, then. That seemed odd. I decided that Mr. Baca was still more interesting than I'd thought. As a matter of fact, I began to wonder a little if I hadn't imagined it all, because Mr. Baca certainly gave not the remotest indication that he had ever seen or heard of the Englishman before. I'm afraid Colonel Arbuthnot-Howe's smile more or less indicated that he thought so too—that I'd imagined it all, I mean.

Dinner was a very diverting affair. Colonel Arbuthnot-Howe had been all over the world, it turned out, and had seen a lot. He had as much charm and polish in his way as Mr. Baca had in his. He was of course intensely British, Baca intensely Southern. But they hit it off beautifully. Did I notice, or did I imagine, that there was a steely quality in the Englishman's blue eyes when Baca wasn't looking at him? I thought he was doing his best to recognize him.

Dinner was almost over when something happened that convinced me that I had been perfectly right about Baca. Miss Carter, with all the tact of the perfect hostess, turned to Colonel Arbuthnot-Howe and asked him if he'd been in Mexico or in the great ranching districts of New Mexico and Arizona.

I was sitting next to Sebastien Baca, and at the question I felt him stiffen with the clarity of an electric shock. It's difficult to explain; but I actually felt the tenseness that he concealed outwardly with perfect urbanity. His spoon didn't so much as touch his tall sherbet glass, and his manner as he waited for the Colonel's answer was only politely interested.

"Yes, I have, Miss Carter, a number of times—in one capacity or another."

He smiled as he said it, leaving us to guess what we would.

"As a matter of fact I'm rather interested in that country. The British Red Cross is trying to buy a large tract of land there for the hospitalization of tuberculosis cases. Our climate is so beastly wretched, you know. I've just been taking it up with your State Department."

"What do they think of it?" asked Thorn, sitting next to him.

"Not bad, you know. Of course, we'd have all sorts of immigration and deportation provisions in any arrangement."

"I think it's a lousy idea," Susan observed without rancour.

"Susan!" said Miss Carter.

"I do. We've got enough t.b.'s in the country without importing them. Why here in Maryland we've got a town *named* T.B.—did you know that, Uncle? It's down in Southern Maryland. I saw it the other day when I was going to Leonardtown."

The conversation turned off on odd names and English pronunciation and the like, until Miss Carter rose and we women left the men to pre-war port from Mr. Sutton's New York stock and whatever tales they chose to tell. They must have been amusing, because we could hear them laughing from on the porch where we had coffee.

Later Dr. Knox dropped in. After a while Dan got out a

36

bridge table in the back parlor, and Miss Carter and Ben went in to play with him and Sue.

Colonel Arbuthnot-Howe was sitting next to me on the swinging bench. Dr. Knox and Mr. Sutton were walking up and down on the terrace. We could follow them by the intermittent glow of their cigars. Mr. Baca and Wally had got very clubby since Wally's awful exhibition of boredom at lunch and were—I suspect—having a drink somewhere. Bill and Thorn were talking in low earnest tones across the verandah.

"Was I right or wrong?" I asked, turning to my companion.

He blew a long fragrant meditative puff from his cigarette and shook his head.

"I was a little embarrassed," he said after a second, with an engagingly ingenuous frankness, "when Miss Carter asked me if I knew Mexico. I've been avoiding the subject because of what you said."

"You haven't answered my question, of course."

"Maybe not. You see I can't really say. I've seen so many people like him. Not an unusual type, out there."

"Meaning let Mrs. Niles mind her own affairs."

"No indeed, Mrs. Niles. I make it my business to mind other people's affairs. I should hardly condemn it in you."

"Are you a detective?" I asked him abruptly.

He laughed.

"I've been a great many things in my day, Mrs. Niles. Do I look like one?"

I hesitated.

"Not entirely," I admitted. "I think it's probably Mr. Baca."

He looked quickly at me, inquiringly.

"I don't mean that he looks like a detective. But I think he looks very much like somebody a detective might be after. And of course, you just sort of *arrived*, you see."

He grinned.

"I do see. Sort of like a story book."

"Precisely," I returned. I didn't know how true his words were.

VIII

Looking back on that evening, it seems strange that we didn't see that something serious was about to happen. Not that there was anything very definite, except perhaps the accident to Sebastien Baca, if indeed you could call that definite.

There was one other thing that did seem strange to me too, even then. But mostly it was just that everything was out of joint someway.

The accident to Mr. Baca was rather surprising.

It must have been about ten o'clock when Bill suggested we go for a swim. It was a gorgeous soft moonlight night, early enough in the season so that the water hadn't got lukewarm and full of sea nettles.

Dr. Knox offered to take Susan's hand at bridge so she could go along. Miss Carter protested mildly—she doesn't approve of night swimming, nor of Dr. Knox's bridge—but she was overruled at once, as always, by everybody. Mr. Sutton clinched the matter by taking Dan's hand and telling us to run along.

About half-way down the linden avenue to the river we came on Wally and Mr. Baca sitting on a marble bench under a light at the side of the path. Wally was hunched forward, when I first saw him, his head in his hands, his ordinarily sleek hair unpleasantly ruffled. The Mexican was sitting beside him, his long legs crossed elegantly, nonchalantly smoking a cigarette. He saw us first and spoke to Wally, who straightened up at once, pushed his hair back into place and got up.

"Hullo," said Bill. "We're swimming. Want to come along?"

I thought Wally looked a little displeased; but Mr. Baca was as charmed as always, and they came along with us.

The bathing pier at Seaton Hall is as elaborately complete, under the guise of being all very simple, as that of any beach club in the world, I suppose. One of the boys turned on the great lights that make it as bright as midday for blocks around and draw every mosquito and assorted insect in the entire river. We separated into the pavilion, where there were bathing suits of every size, color and style to fit the largest impromptu party.

"I wonder if Montezuma can swim," Susan remarked, slipping her smooth wavy hair into a green rubber turban.

"All snakes can swim," replied Thorn coolly. "Look at Cousin Wally."

Susan, not having had much to take off and considerably less to put on, was all ready. She perched her slim figure perilously on a towel rack and regarded Thorn with exasperating superiority.

"It must be ghastly to be in love," she said calmly. "Thorn's been a perfect pig all day. All because good old Franklin has gone back home. I'm going to ask Uncle to retain him to

38

fight the service station. Keep him in town so the rest of us can have some peace."

"You'll do nothing of the sort," Thorn retorted hotly.

"Sha'n't I just. Only first I'm going swimming. Look, Martha—she actually wears a slip. No wonder it takes her forever to get ready."

We joined the men on the pier, where Susan regarded her uncle's guests with the practised and severe eye of a stockman appraising cattle.

"They'll do," she whispered to us.

"Let's have the lights off, Dan," Thorn said, ignoring her. "These bugs are beastly. It's almost as light without them. Anyway, the only thing to remember to keep away from is out in the middle. There's a bad current. Right, Dan?"

"Okay. Okay, Bill?"

Bill nodded and went in the pavilion. In a second the lights were out and Seaton River turned from a dark glittering sheet to a multitude of glistening lapping little waves rustling forward to break lightly against the wall.

Susan, first in as always, looked like something from another world, her smooth white arms and slim body moving gracefully out into the pale silver night.

"It's swell," she called. "Come along, Bill, I'll race you to the raft."

Bill dived in, and in a minute all of us were in, laughing, shouting, splashing on our way out to the raft and diving towers.

Mr. Baca turned out to be a marvellous swimmer. He and Wally, who seemed to get back his spirits as soon as he hit the water—if indeed I was right in thinking he'd lost them before—did some almost breath-taking stunts. Mr. Baca's glistening swan dive was the loveliest thing of its kind I'd ever seen. I gathered from Susan's comments, not knowing authoritatively about it myself, that Colonel Arbuthnot-Howe, while he swam well enough, wasn't quite as much at home in the water as the others, especially Wally and Mr. Baca. Those two, with Bill and Susan, kept making rapid excursions out into the river, where we could only see an occasional arm flash in the pale light and disappear. Suddenly they'd turn up almost at the raft and disappear again under the surface for what seemed impossible lengths of time, and bob up again with a shout yards and yards away. At first Dan, Thorn, Colonel Arbuthnot-Howe and I watched their antics with an admiring derision. Finally we lost interest and amused ourselves with the polo ball and some less spectacular diving.

39

I was beginning to get a little chillier than I like to be when I heard the great clock of St. Margaret's strike the half hour.

"I'm going in, Thorn," I called.

"Me too," said Dan. We climbed up on the pier together.

It occurred suddenly to Susan that we ought to have something hot to drink sent down from the house.

"Who'll have soup, coffee or Scotch?" she called out to the rest of them still in the water.

"Soup!" shouted Bill promptly.

"Scotch!" shouted Wally and Colonel Arbuthnot-Howe.

"Coffee for me," I said, and Dan and Thorn joined in with me.

"What about you, Mr. Baca?" She looked about.

That was the first time any of us had missed him.

I don't know why I, and apparently the others too, just assumed that something had happened to him. Maybe it was Susan herself. She stood stock still on the pier, staring out over the gently moving water. Her little hands were clenched tightly. I could see the fear gradually growing on her that I felt myself.

"Mr. Baca!" she called.

There was no answer.

"He's probably gone out in the river again, 'sall," Bill put in, unconvincingly I'm afraid. At any rate he followed it with a shout: "Baca!"

We waited in dead silence. There was no sound but the lap lap of the waves against the wall. Someone else called; this time we heard a faint hollow mocking echo from the other shore.

Then Colonel Arbuthnot-Howe put his hands to his mouth and shouted "Ho! Baca! Baca!" It seemed that only the dead could fail to hear that colossal roar. Again the hollow "baca baca" from across the river.

"If he can't hear that he's out on the Russian steppes," Susan said. All her usual levity was in her voice, but I could feel her frightened anxiety.

"Turn on the lights, Dan," Bill said quietly. "I'll get the boat. The rest of you had better get dressed."

"I'll go with you," Susan said quickly.

"You get dressed. We'll take care of this."

They got out the boat. Thorn stood on the edge of the pier without saying a word. When Bill and Dan came around she jumped lightly down.

"I'm going along," she said. "Head straight out; if he got in the current he may be on the shoal . . . like Agnes."

40

That's all I heard as they slipped quickly away from the pier.

Susan turned to me. Her face was curiously grave and a little bewildered.

"What's the matter with Thorn?" she asked. "I've never seen her stir herself before, no matter how many people were getting drowned."

Wally and Arbuthnot-Howe were still on the pier with us. My teeth were chattering violently, although I really wasn't very cold.

"You'd better get dressed, Mrs. Niles," Colonel Arbuthnot-Howe said. "Fenton and I will see about the first aid kit."

Wally started as if he had suddenly waked up. "Of course," he said quickly. "Stupid of me—I'll get it. Got a cigarette, anybody?"

Susan handed him a limp package of Camels out of the pocket of her robe. I glanced at her. She was watching Wally's shaking trembling fingers, trying to extract a cigarette, with an expression of complete contempt on her curled lips. Suddenly she looked at the Englishman, who was looking gravely out in the direction in which the boat had gone.

"I'm going to get dressed," she said shortly, and went inside.

"What about this, Mrs. Niles—is it dangerous out there? Miss Thorn said there was a current?"

"It's not dangerous if he does hit the current," I said. "For the simple reason that it will force him onto the shoal or into the crab grass—unless he hits it too far down. It's funny, he's such a splendid swimmer. He's probably just out there somewhere, having a good time by himself."

But I didn't believe what I was saying, and neither did the Englishman.

"You'd better dress before you take cold," he said, tossing his cigarette butt into the river. I heard it strike the water with a sharp sizzle and go out.

IX

I went into the bath house to get dressed. Susan was sitting on a three-legged stool carefully flicking cigarette ash into the little puddle of water forming on the floor by her wet sandals.

41

"What's the matter with you?" I asked, shaking out my hair that someway always manages to get wet no matter what kind of a cap I wear.

"Nothing."

Obviously there was something. The mere fact of Susan's sitting by herself when there were people ten yards away from her was sufficient evidence, even if I hadn't seen her deadly serious young face.

"He'll be all right."

"It's funny though, do you know, Martha," she answered without looking up.

"Why?"

"Because."

"You're too definite."

"I mean it's funny they haven't found him."

"Why?"

"Because."

I finished my shower, put on my clothes and pinned up my hair. Still she said nothing.

"You're like Falstaff," I said at last. "If reasons were as thick as blackberries you wouldn't give any under compulsion. I'm going out. You can sit here as long as you like."

"Did you see him swim? And then I think it's funny because this is what happened to Agnes last year."

"What do you mean?" I stared in amazement at her. "You're not pretending that just because you have two accidents in two years they're in any way connected, are you? When you think of the hundreds of people who've been swimming off this pier, it's much funnier, as you call it, that you don't have more of this sort of thing."

She mumbled something under her breath. I think she was about to be more coherent about it when we heard a shout from Colonel Arbuthnot-Howe. Both of us ran outside.

We saw the boat coming swiftly toward us and watched breathlessly while Dan swerved in and straightened his bow, bringing the light boat flush against the dock. Sebastien Baca was lying perfectly still in the bottom.

"He's all right," Dan shouted. "Give a hand, Arbuthnot."

They lifted the limp form of the Mexican to the float and carried him up on the pier. Colonel Arbuthnot-Howe somehow seemed to take charge without a word. He listened for a second with his head at Baca's chest and felt his pulse. The rest of us stood stock still watching him. He turned Baca on his stomach and began the rhythmic raising and lowering of his torso. He seemed so enormously capable and professional

42

about it—as if he had resuscitated thousands of drowned people.

It seemed ages, and probably was a minute or two, before he straightened up, a grave smile on his lips.

"He's coming along. Have you got some spirits here?"

Thorn took the brandy bottle that Wally had brought from the pavilion medicine chest and handed it to him. He turned the Mexican over on his back, raised his head and poured a few drops into his mouth. Sebastien Baca's eyelids flickered.

"Good man," said Colonel Arbuthnot-Howe quietly.

The Mexican's eyes opened their full width for one instant, and he smiled faintly.

"Gracias!" he whispered.

They laid him down again. He seemed entirely exhausted.

"We've got to get him to the house," Thorn said. "What's the best way?"

She turned to Dan, who was standing a little to one side, his arms folded, looking down at the Mexican.

If I hadn't had ample proof of Dan's good sense in the six years I'd known him, I should have thought that like Susan he was seeing something "funny" about this too. He was so obviously puzzled about something, looking down at Mr. Baca with the queerest expression on his face. At Thorn's question he glanced up sharply.

"Sure," he said, as though he hadn't until then thought there was anything else to do. "I'll phone Matthews to send my car down. That's quickest."

They took Sebastien Baca to the house in the rumble seat of Dan's Cadillac roadster, all wrapped up in blankets and robes from the pavilion. Bill and Dan and Thorn went with him. Wally and the colonel walked up to the house with Susan and me.

We didn't say anything until about half way up the linden avenue. Then Colonel Arbuthnot-Howe, who had been working abstractedly with a funny stump of pipe that wouldn't draw, said abruptly, "The bruise on the fellow's cheek is rather odd, what, Fenton?"

"What bruise?" Susan said quickly. But not quickly enough to keep me from hearing Wally's sharp intake of breath.

I glanced at him. In the bluish light of the high moon his face was ghastly. It isn't a strong face at best; at worst, as I saw it that instant, it was unbelievably weak, contorted, almost, with something so close to sheer terror that it was almost indecent. I'm afraid the tree-shaded streets and faded mauve façades of our tiny Georgian town sap one's capacity for anything very primitive in the way of human emotions. We like such things covered up. I suppose if I'd known that Wally was suffering some horrible revulsion but keeping his mask in place, I'd have been alarmed maybe; at any rate I'd have been terribly sorry for him. As it was, my feeling was exactly as if the Reverend Lucius Button, the fundamentalist of Landover, had appeared on York Road naked. It was not only indecent. In some way it was revolting.

"Didn't you notice?" Arbuthnot-Howe said in some surprise. "Of course I may be quite wrong, you know," he added hastily.

Wally had recovered himself in the merciful shadows of the lindens.

"I thought I noticed something too," he said. "I wasn't sure of it though. Dan says they found him on the shoal. Tide out, fortunately. He must have run on a pile out there."

Susan was silent, odd as that was. Colonel Arbuthnot-Howe said "No doubt." We went on to the house.

Miss Carter luckily had gone to bed. Luckily, because we should have had to listen to a lecture on the dangers of night bathing, for which I think we all preferred to wait until morning. And no one else was particularly disturbed. After all, it was just one of those things, and the man wasn't drowned. Mr. Sutton and Dr. Knox were in the library, talking, as they always talked, about the college, its endowment fund, its lacrosse team, its ancient past and its hopes and fears for tomorrow. That's one nice thing about a college. Its future is always so important, an eternally intriguing problem. My husband and Mr. Sutton's secretary, a serious young man from Princeton whose life was made a constant torment by Susan, were playing chess on the bridge table in the back drawing room.

"I suppose some one has called Mac?" Mr. Sutton remarked casually.

"I suppose so," I said. "Mac" is Dr. McPherson, our cloud by day and pillar of fire by night.

I went out into the hall, and just then Thorn came down stairs. Her eyes were like black caverns against the deathly pallor of her face. The uneven remnants of lipstick gave her mouth a curiously twisted look—or perhaps it *was* twisted.

"Where's Uncle?" she said, in a tense effort to control herself.

"In the library. How's Mr. Baca?"

She shrugged her shoulders.

"He'll be all right. Dan called Dr. Mac, but he's out in

44

the country having a baby. Dan got him on the phone, though, and found out what to do. Is Uncle Dan alone?"

"Dr. Knox is in there. They're talking about the college."

Thorn made a sound that was somewhere between a sob and a laugh.

"Whether to have a training table or a chemistry laboratory, I suppose."

"You'd better go to bed," I said. "Ben and Matthew are in the middle of something, but as Susan's in there I imagine they'll be glad to call it off. Really, Thorn, you must go to bed."

She shook her head.

"Not until I've seen Uncle."

I knew there wasn't any use trying to reason with her. I got my wrap and finally my husband and we started home.

"I hope Mr. Baca doesn't get pneumonia," I remarked as we went down the steps. But Ben wasn't listening. He muttered something about knights, queens, checkmating and Susan. I gathered that if Susan got pneumonia it would be a boon to chess-players and we let it go at that.

Tim Healy came out of his lodge when we got to the gate. The Suttons keep it closed at night. "Good night to you both," he said. "It's a rare foine night but there's showers ahead. Night to you, sir; good night, Ma'am."

Ben was still thinking about his interrupted chess, or maybe about something else. Anyway, he wasn't talking. He added a perfunctory "Good night" to my cordial one, and we went out into York Road.

Across the street most of Landover College was asleep. An occasional light in Taney Hall, and the far-off strumming of a banjo were the only evidence that four hundred young men were tucked away behind the leafy screen of tulip poplars, and elms and ivy. Dr. Knox's house was dark except for the dim fan light over the door. There's something very moving about a college campus late at night. I felt it now; and I half turned to glance back at the other thing on York Road that always moves me too—Aunt Charlotte's white-washed cabin, with its ancient fence and the hollyhocks moving rigidly, like thin sentinels, in the luminous blue moonlight.

Everything was so calm out there. The campus, the trees along York Road, the high brick wall with its overhanging clusters of purple and white lilacs. Tim back in his lodge, lighting his pipe and reading a chapter in the Bible, waiting to close the gate; Aunt Charlotte down the road asleep. Aunt Charlotte remembered the old soldiers who had been quartered down the river when she was a girl. Those old soldiers had fought in the Revolution. Lord! I thought, and Susan doesn't remember the World War, and thinks Colonel Arbuthnot-Howe is old.

We were turning in our own gate when I thought I heard something down King Charles Street. Normally, I suppose, one expects to hear sounds on streets; but never in Landover after midnight. At any rate, noises after that time are unusual enough so that I was justifiably curious. I stepped back and glanced down King Charles Street. To my astonishment I recognized, scurrying along close to the Suttons' wall, the absurd figure of Reverdy Hawkins, the colored lawyer. He stopped under the old-fashioned street lamp—which we still affect in Landover—and glanced back cautiously. I saw him reach in his pocket, bring out something and examine it closely. He put his thumb to his mouth, and began, as nearly as I could see, counting something that he held in his hand. There was no doubt what it was that he was counting. That in itself was surprising, and the hour made it more so. But it was still more surprising because no one ever uses the great barred gate on King Charles Street.

X

The grotesque top-hatted figure of Reverdy Hawkins greedily counting his money under the dim lamp in King Charles Street, at one o'clock in the morning, would, ordinarily, have been rather comical. As it was, against the background of the last fifteen hours, it was decidedly sinister. There was something furtive about it. Furthermore, I knew only too well how dangerous the most harmless person can get when he is in the clutches of cupidity. I went to sleep thinking that somebody might as well have given a child a stick of dynamite. And I'm afraid there wasn't much doubt in my mind who, in this instance, that somebody was.

I didn't, of course, mention any of this to my husband. His curiosity is peculiarly limited. He will dig in the sand or crawl through caves on hands and knees for three months on end in the most torrid weather, to find out what kind of hair ornaments middle-class ladies wore during the Third Crô-Magnon Dynasty. In the domestic affairs of his contemporaries, however, he has the most profound absence of interest. Until I learned better I used to burst in on him with some astounding piece of gossip, such as that the wife of the

French professor had refused to return the call of the wife of the Mathematics professor—and be received with that polite but so uninterested "Oh?" that Americans learn at Oxford. Gradually I've learned to ponder on the ways and affairs of faculty wives in silence, or at least to more sympathetic ears.

I suppose I was asleep as soon as I put my head on my pillow, and I have a vague memory of dreaming that some one was calling me; and that became so insistent that at last I woke up and lay there listening. I glanced at my clock. The radium hands showed 2:15. I turned over and closed my eyes. Then I sat up. I heard the far-off buzz of the front door bell —it sounds in the kitchen—and heard my name: "Martha!" I think I knew what Thorn Carter wanted before I got into my dressing gown and went down to open the door.

She was standing there much as she had stood in the hall at home a few hours before. But she seemed paler. Her body swayed a little, as if the effort to stay erect was almost more than she could bear.

She came in slowly. I had the feeling when she did that she realized how futile it was for one human being ever to come to another with a burden. She probably felt that just getting away from one place to another would change something that ached inside of her. But it's something I imagine we all have to learn sometime, that we take our heartaches with us. I know I felt horribly helpless just then. I wanted to tell her there was nothing she could do but wait. I suppose heartaches do fade and lose their sharp edges in time—at least people say that.

We sat down on the living room sofa. I at one end, she at the other.

"What's the matter, Thorn?"

"Uncle," she said dully. "I did talk to him. He's going to change his will, tomorrow."

"Did he tell you that?"

She shook her head.

"No. He didn't."

She was staring straight ahead, hopeless tears welling up in her eyes, her voice tight and clipped.

"I heard him tell Dr. Knox that he was getting Mr. Rand down to-morrow. He telephoned for him. He's coming at noon."

"That doesn't necessarily mean he's changing his will," I said. I knew however that it probably did mean just that.

She took a long deep breath and closed her eyes.

"Yes. They'd been talking about it. I know they had, because they want him down for a college Board meeting next week and they were trying to save him a trip. Uncle let Dr. Knox out and said 'You'll be over to lunch.' "

"That doesn't seem to concern you."

"It does though. I met Uncle Dan coming back. Susan had gone upstairs. He was out quite a little while, talking to Tim, I guess, and he came in smiling. I'd rather die than see him smile. It was awful, awful."

Her voice was intense with tears. She pulled painfully at the sodden little handkerchief in her hands.

"Thorn!" I said. "For God's sake pull yourself together!"

"Oh, it was terrible! He didn't see me at first, and when he did he just sort of laughed. I said 'Uncle Dan, listen to me, I've got to marry Franklin—I don't care whether you change your will or not.' "

I stared at the girl. She was almost beside herself. I thought it was best to let her talk it out.

"He laughed. He said 'I'll change my will a plenty and don't you forget it. Marry him if you please. Do any damn fool thing you want to: only don't cry to me about it.' Then he walked into the library and slammed the door. I couldn't bear it, Martha! I sat down on the steps and cried. He didn't come out. After a while I went up stairs."

She was talking by now in jerky little gasps, now and then punctuating by pounding the cushions with a tightly closed fist.

"I lay down on my bed and tried to tell myself how stupid I was—that it didn't matter, that Franklin doesn't care or he'd call me up or something, that I'd got to snap out of it. I went to sleep. Then I woke up, I'd thought I heard something."

"Where?"

"Down stairs. I got up and went out and looked over the bannister."

"Did you see anything?"

"No, it was pitch dark. But I did hear something more. First I thought it was in the library. Maybe it was Uncle Dan, but there wasn't any light anywhere."

"What did you do?"

"I just listened. I wasn't frightened, then. I guess I was too tired to be frightened."

She sounded like a little girl wistfully apologizing for something quite sweet that she'd done.

"I stayed there a long time. Then I thought I'd wake one of the boys. Wally's room was nearest, so I tipped over to the door and opened it as quietly as I could. It was very dark and

I didn't want to turn on the light, so I went over to his bed and touched his shoulder—but he wasn't there. I felt the bed —it was turned down of course, but it was all smooth, nobody had slept in it."

"What did you do then?"

"Then I got frightened. You know what Wally's like. I went back and put on these tennis slippers and this coat and tip-toed down stairs. I couldn't see anybody but I *knew* somebody was there—and it didn't *feel* like anybody I knew."

"What do you mean?"

"I mean . . . you know . . . how you sense people you know even in the dark. I suppose it's a sort of instinct—isn't it?—or smell, or characteristic sound. You know what I mean. Anyway, I felt somebody was there and I didn't know him. I mean it wasn't Wally or . . . Uncle Dan."

"Didn't you turn on the lights?"

She shook her head slowly and caught her under lip between her teeth with a sharp intake of breath.

"I was afraid," she said quietly. "I *knew* that whoever it was was by the light switch. And . . . well, I didn't want him to touch me . . . that's all."

I looked at her intently. I was wide awake by this time, and I kept listening to Thorn's story—although of course at that time I had no idea of the importance it took on in view of what was happening—in fact had already happened— with peculiar intensity. And somehow, without my being able either then or now to say why it was, I felt absolutely certain that Thorn Carter was deliberately lying to me. I looked away quickly. Then it occurred to me that perhaps she was lying to herself too.

"What did you do then, Thorn?" I asked in as matter-of-fact a voice as I could.

"When I got to the bottom of the stairs I thought I'd go to the back drawing room and go out through a window and get Tim. I got as far as the door and I saw that the garden door was open. I ran outside. Then I heard someone coming. I guess I lost my head then; I ran around the kitchen and down the road to the King Charles Street gate and over here."

By this time Thorn as well as myself was curiously calm about all this business. Our eyes met; I think we understood each other. I hesitated a moment before asking my next question. Then I decided it would be just as well to get it over with.

"Thorn," I said, "how did you get out of the King Charles gate? Wasn't it locked?"

She looked at me blankly for a second, perfectly silent and apparently bewildered. I saw her bite her lower lip again. It was a mannerism that both she and Dan had when puzzled or annoyed.

"I hadn't thought of that, Martha."

"Did you know it was open? It's always locked, isn't it?"

She nodded slowly.

"Yes. It's always locked. I wonder what I was thinking of."

She stared straight ahead of her. Then she said abruptly, "I'm going back, Martha. You've got to come with me."

I looked at her, trying to fathom what lay behind her sudden determination to go back, and what lay behind her change from hysterical child to self-controlled woman. I got a coat out of the hall closet and slipped it on. One of the children's flashlights was on the floor by his small rubbers, and I put it in my pocket. I switched out the lights and we went out.

"Let's go back through the King Charles gate," I whispered when we came to the corner. I thought she hesitated an instant. Perhaps I imagined it. Anyway, we went swiftly down the street, passing under the dim lamp where I'd seen Reverdy Hawkins counting his bills an hour or so before. We stopped at the great iron grill. I pushed it. It didn't open. I looked at Thorn. She gave it a harder push. Still it didn't budge. I took the flashlight from my pocket and turned it on the huge lock.

Thorn and I stared at each other in the darkness. The King Charles gate was bolted and locked, just as it always is.

XI

"But it was open a minute ago," Thorn whispered, gripping my arm convulsively.

"It isn't now."

"But Martha, who could have done it?"

I shrugged my shoulders. I was skeptical of the whole business. Convinced as I was that Thorn hadn't been telling the truth—at least not the whole truth—a few moments before, it didn't take much to make me doubt anything she said. Especially anything as preposterous as this. Still there was genuine alarm in her voice and in those tight fingers on my arm.

"We'll go around the other way," I said, "and wake up Tim—if he's not already awake."

She nodded. We turned back along King Charles Street in the shadow of the long brick wall. As we passed again under the lamp post where Reverdy had stood I noticed suddenly a piece of paper lying on the brick walk. I reached down in the dim yellow light and picked it up.

"What's that?" Thorn asked quickly.

"It looks like a piece of paper."

I stuffed it in my coat pocket, wondering if by chance Reverdy had dropped it when he brought his roll of bills out to count them under the light.

It occurred to me then that someone in Seaton Hall might have left the gate unlocked so that Reverdy could leave the grounds. Supposing that whoever it was wanted to avoid any possible chance of being seen with the Negro lawyer, he—or she—might conceivably have left the gate unlocked, then when everybody was in bed, come down and locked it. That would explain the time from one o'clock when I heard the click of the gate and saw Reverdy under the lamp, until Thorn came that way at 2:15.

"Thorn," I said as we turned down York Road towards the main gate, "did you hear anyone near the gate when you came through?"

"No," she said slowly, "and yes."

She hesitated a second before she explained. "I was running along the road. I thought I heard someone after me. But I thought it was just my imagination. The faster I ran the more frightened I was. It may have been someone. I wasn't sure."

I thought that was reasonable enough. Isn't there—wasn't there when I was in college—a theory in psychology that you are afraid because you run, and not that you run because you are afraid? That would explain Thorn's fogginess about it. There was only one thing it didn't explain. I wondered vaguely about it for a second as we went along; then suddenly it came quite clearly to me.

"Are you sure you came through that gate?" I asked abruptly.

It was quite dark now. When I looked at her I couldn't make out anything clearly, except the white blur of her face and neck. She didn't answer at once. Then she said in a calm unruffled voice, "Yes, Martha. I'm sure. Why? Don't you believe me?"

I'd never make a good diplomat—as Ben has several times observed. I can't ever see the good of beating about the bush, and I've never learned when it's best to leave something unsaid. On this case—as usual—I regretted my reply as soon as I'd made it.

"It just seems strange to me that you'd come that way at all. It's always locked. How did you expect to get out? What I mean is . . ."

"I know what you mean, Martha," she interrupted me quietly. "You mean I must have expected to find the gate open. Or even that I knew the gate was open. Otherwise I'd obviously have gone the other way, because we all know that gate's always locked. That's what you mean—isn't it?"

"Exactly," I said.

She didn't say anything for a minute. We were walking rapidly along York Road. It wasn't until we got to the main gate, and she had pressed the bell to wake Tim, that she said, "You're quite right, Martha. I did expect to find the gate open."

That was all. No explanation, nothing. I could think what I pleased for the time being. And I did. I thought of the figure in the yellow lamp-light, the slip of paper in my pocket, Mr. Sutton's accusation of some member of his own family, earlier in the evening.

Perhaps it was the nature of my thoughts that made the time seem interminable before the latch went click-click-click and Thorn pushed open the little iron grill at the right of the great gate. We went in.

"It's us, Tim," Thorn called as we passed under his window. "Too sleepy even to be angry," she added to me when he didn't open the window and deliver the usual tirade on burning the candle at both ends and turning God's blessed night into day. Poor old Tim! There must be holy angels somewhere for people who believed in them with such childlike faith as Tim's.

At that moment neither of us was particularly concerned with Tim, and we went quickly up the drive, turning to the left of the box screen into the area in front of the Hall.

"Look!" Thorn whispered suddenly; "there's a light!" She broke into a run up the steps and peered in the long window at the side of the door. I followed her, and looked over her shoulder. The hall chandelier was lighted, but the hall was empty.

"We'd better go around," she said. "I don't want to wake Lafayette."

For some quite hidden reason I put my hand on the great brass knob and turned it gently. I don't think I in the least expected it to open; I've never known the front door of

52

Seaton Hall to be unlocked. Maybe it was simply because everything was out of joint that I thought this might be too. In any case, the knob turned and the great door swung back as I pushed it open. Thorn and I looked at each other without a word. There was no doubting that she was completely bewildered by what in any other place than Daniel Sutton's household would seem an ordinary inefficiency on some servant's part.

We stepped into the dimly lighted, ghastly silent hall. All of our senses were heightened, I imagine; I noticed a curious dry, faintly pungent odor that I'd never noticed before; I even noticed, I remember, several crystals missing on the candelabra, and the stain on the ceiling that was made when Susan left the tap on upstairs and the gardener turned off the sprinklers in the garden.

Thorn suddenly clutched at my arm. I heard a faint sound, of someone moving back and forth. I even thought I heard the rustle of papers. Then everything was silent again. We waited breathlessly. I heard the noise again. I felt Thorn's grip on my arm relax.

"It's Uncle Dan," she whispered, although the need for whispering, I thought, should be over.

We went a little further into the hall, quietly, until I could see the library door set in its deep frame. It was ajar about six inches. I went back and closed the hall door. Mr. Sutton was moving back and forth. I heard him move back a chair, and I heard the low buzz of the phone. I heard him speak; that is I heard the sound of his voice, though I couldn't make out any words.

Thorn took hold of my arm again. It was decidedly reassuring, someway, to know that we weren't the only people awake and moving in the great downstairs rooms with their reverberating echoes of a hundred and sixty years of generations of children, men and women. As a matter of fact, in view of what the next half-hour was to bring, I can't understand now why instead of being relieved when we heard Mr. Sutton in the library we weren't alarmed. The more I've thought of it the odder it seems.

By this time we were well into the hall. As we got to the foot of the stairs the grandfather clock on the landing whirred and struck three sonorous notes.

"Aren't you going in to see him?" I asked in a low voice.

She shook her head. I could see the old resentment, that had somehow got lost in this half-hour, rising again and increasing in bitterness as it rose.

"No," she said sullenly. "Not tonight. That was Tim on

53

the phone telling him we'd come in. If he'd wanted to see me he'd have come out."

I shrugged my shoulders.

"In that case," I said, "I'm going to see that you get in bed, and then I'm going home. Anybody would think we were two lunatics, wandering about at this time of night and in this garb."

She turned to me with a sort of plea in her voice.

"Why don't you stay all night, Martha? Ben won't even know you've gone."

"I know . . . that's why I'd better go home."

We went upstairs. I sat on a window seat smoking a cigarette while Thorn got ready for bed. I was thinking how much greater the distance between people becomes when they've been very close and something happens to separate them. It's much greater than the distance between casual friends. I suppose it's the law of the pendulum again. Anyway, Thorn was undressing, thinking Heaven knows what. I shudder when I think of what it must have been. I've never discussed it with her since. My own thoughts weren't any too pleasant, and I was getting to the point where I wanted some sleep.

At last she got into the high bed with its lovely carved mahogany posts, drew the covers up around her chin and closed her eyes wearily. I tossed my cigarette into the grate and got up.

"Shall I turn out your light?"

She nodded without opening her eyes. I saw a tear creep out from under the closed lids and run down the side of her cheek, and disappear in the cluster of dark hair at her ear. My emotions about Thorn at the moment were highly mixed. Ordinarily she isn't nervy and she doesn't cry easily, and ordinarily I should have been sympathetic at once, under the circumstances. But now my chief feeling was that she ought to be spanked, that she was making an idiot of herself and keeping me up without any reason whatsoever.

I snapped the light off, said goodnight as sweetly as I could, and started for the door.

"Martha!"

I heard the tight little voice choked out between sobs, and I went over to her bed. She was holding out her hand. I took it.

"Don't be silly," I said gently. "It'll seem better in the morning. Go to sleep."

Her hand clutched mine tightly.

"Listen, Martha."

"What is it?"

"Martha, please, *please* don't think I'm horrible—will you? Promise me you won't."

I was a little alarmed, I may say. I *do* like things to be calm, and I don't like everybody always upset.

"I'll believe anything you tell me, Thorn, unless it's obviously absurd," I said, a little wearily I'm afraid. "Go to sleep, will you?"

"Oh, I can't! I don't think I'll ever go to sleep again. Please don't go."

"All right," I said. I was now becoming a little exasperated. "I'll stay. But first I'm going to get you some hot milk. That'll put you to sleep. I'll stay as long as you want me to."

She nodded wearily and let go my hand. I felt the listless thud of her arm as it dropped at her side. It occurred to me that she'd probably be asleep in two minutes if I left her alone.

I went back to the door and looked out into the hall. The light downstairs was still burning. No one had come upstairs, or we would have heard him. I felt some hesitancy—although not much—at prowling around in Seaton Hall at three o'clock in the morning in a tweed coat, a peach-colored night-dress and a pair of tennis slippers with a ten-cent store flashlight and a piece of dirty paper in my pocket. Nevertheless I decided to go to the kitchen and get Thorn the milk, and then get home if I could before daylight.

I looked down the stair well and decided that the coast was clear enough for me to set out. I wasn't even in danger of being seen from the library; Mr. Sutton had closed the door after Tim had called him. I suppose he probably didn't care to see Thorn any more than she cared to see him. So I went back and closed Thorn's door and started down. Half-way down I stopped dead in my tracks. I heard something, unmistakably, on the other side of the hall—not on the side of the library, where Mr. Sutton was, but across from it. It seemed to come from the back drawing room where Susan had interrupted the game of chess. I listened, absolutely petrified with fear. It was a stealthy, intermittent noise; it seemed to come closer and closer; and the closer it came the more utterly terrified I was. I couldn't scream. I couldn't move. I simply stood there, my gaze rivetted down on the door in the shadow of the stairs at my right. God knows what I expected to see there. I was sick with fear.

Suddenly I simply couldn't stand it another moment. I made some sort of a desperate attempt to scream, but not a sound could I utter. My throat was dumb. Then I burst down the stairs and flew across the hall to the library. I opened the door.

"Mr. Sutton!" I cried, and stopped short. The room was in utter darkness. I stood there, just inside the door, not daring to move forward in the inky darkness or to look back across the dimly lighted hall where I knew something was waiting. I was indescribably terrified. I felt myself swaying, until with a tremendous effort of will I felt along the wall until my numb fingers touched the light switch. I pressed it.

Slowly I turned around then to face the hall and the doorway across it. I caught hold of the back of a high wing chair and leaned against it, waiting, in an agony of suspense. The great house was as silent as an empty grave, with the pulse of time beating eternally against it: tick, tock; tick, tock; tick, tock. It seemed to me, standing there, gripping the soft brocatelle, that something horrible must come through that door, and that I mustn't move until it came. Tick, tock; tick, tock; tick, tock: the horrible deliberateness of the clock was unbearable. Gradually and slowly I relaxed my grip on the chair and let my hand drop, until . . . I shrieked and turned . . . and raised my hand dripping with blood. I stared at it like a maniac, and then at the thing it had touched. It was Daniel Sutton, sitting in that chair. He was dead, the blood still wet on the glazed surface of his shirt front, still slowly dripping from the ghastly cavern in his head.

I stood still. A terrible nauseating wave flowed over me. I didn't see Colonel Arbuthnot-Howe when he came into the room; but I saw him just as I lost all consciousness, and I knew he caught me when I fell.

XII

I don't know how long I was unconscious. I seemed lost in one of those infinite wells of time. It couldn't have been more than a few seconds, because Colonel Arbuthnot-Howe was still holding me, and wiping the cold viscid wet crimson smear from my fingers. And as I came to I heard the other steps on the landing. The Englishman with a grim friendly smile said "Steady on, there's a stout fella," as Dan and Bill burst into the room.

"What's up?" Dan said, staring at me.

He couldn't see behind the high shielding back of the wing chair. All that he and Bill could see was my outlandish coat

56

over my nightdress and my tennis slippers, and the blood on the handkerchief in Colonel Arbuthnot-Howe's hand.

He stepped forward.

"There's been an accident, I'm afraid, Sutton," he said steadily.

Then Dan saw what I hadn't seen, the limp hand hanging over the short arm of the chair. It all happened in a flash: his seeing the hand, then seeing his father, then knowing that he was dead.

"Dad!" he said.

Bill was just behind him. I couldn't see their faces. I didn't want to. I couldn't avoid seeing the sudden slump in their young shoulders, and Bill's arm go over Dan's shoulder, and hear Dan saying huskily "Steady, old son." I saw Colonel Arbuthnot-Howe turn away, and I saw him straighten suddenly. I followed his gaze to the door.

It was Susan. She stood there in a long yellow negliée, pushing her tangled yellow mop of hair from her flushed sleepy face.

"What's the ghastly row about?" she demanded drowsily.

Then she saw me and wrinkled her forehead. Gradually it dawned on her that something was wrong.

"What's the matter?" she said sharply, wide awake now. "Did he die?"

Even Colonel Arbuthnot-Howe started.

"Who, Miss Atwood?" he asked quietly.

"Mr. Baca, of course."

She looked in bewilderment from one of us to the other. I had to remind myself that she also couldn't see Mr. Sutton from where she stood.

It was our turn to be astonished. Bill left his brother and went to the door.

"What makes you think of Mr. Baca, Sue?" he asked gently.

"Because he was up. I saw him out of my window about two, or a little after. I just thought something had happened to him—that's all."

"It's not Baca, Sue," Bill said with a little gulp. "It's Dad. He's dead . . . shot."

She took it very well. Her face grew pale, she closed her eyes a second, then opened them and put her hand on Bill's arm.

"I'm sorry, Bill," she whispered. "Dear Uncle Dan."

Tears came to my eyes. I think it was the sweetest epitaph · Daniel Sutton had.

A deep sob shook Bill's shoulders, and he bowed his head

for an instant. Then he said, "We'll have to get Dr. Mac, Dan."

Dan came over to Susan too.

"Go upstairs, Sue, will you? You'd better tell Thorn and Aunt Mildred. I'll call Sullivan. Will you stay here, Arbuthnot? Don't touch anything and don't let anybody in."

Colonel Arbuthnot-Howe nodded. He had been glancing around the room. I caught, or thought I caught, a steely flicker in his eyes when Susan said she'd seen the Mexican from her window. There was something rather reassuring about his large figure in striped pajamas and camel's-hair dressing gown. At least there was until I happened to look at his feet. He had on rubber-soled shoes.

I'm afraid I stared at them longer than I should have done. When I glanced up he was looking at me with a quizzical semi-smile on his bronzed face.

"Well?" he asked in an undertone. "What do you make of it?"

"It just looks funny, that's all," I said feebly.

"It is, rather, isn't it?" he smiled, and let it go at that. In a moment Dan came back.

"I think we'll get out of here and go in the parlor," he said. "Sullivan will be over in a minute."

He looked at me. A curious expression came into his eyes. I think he just that instant realized that there was anything unusual about my being there. Even then the grotesqueness of my costume didn't strike him.

He closed the door after us, put the key in the lock and turned it. Then he put the key in his pocket and we went across the hall. I hesitated involuntarily before I stepped into that room. The few seconds on the stairs were still too vivid in my mind, in spite of what I had seen in the library.

Dan snapped on the light.

"Hello!" he exclaimed. "What's this?"

Curiosity overcame what reluctance I felt about going in there. I looked between the two men and saw what had surprised Dan. One of the long windows opening out on the porch was open. The gauze curtain was billowing gently in the breeze. I shivered convulsively.

"I guess we'd better keep out of here too," Dan said quietly. We went out into the hall. Just then the doorbell rang and Dr. Mac came in. I think all of us had the feeling that everything would be much better now that he was there. Dr. Mac is getting too stout now—he puffs when he walks up stairs—and they say he drinks more port than he should; but for all that his kindly grey eyes see through every pain you ever have, and his medicine, whether it's something bitter out of a bottle or something healing in his soul, never fails the people of Landover. He came in and set his bag down.

"What's the trouble?" he asked, and then saw me, shivering behind the big Englishman.

"Whatever it is, you go home, Martha, and go to bed," he said. Because we're all used to obeying him, I nodded at once.

Dan looked at me, trying vaguely to figure out how I came to be there. I think he wanted to ask me, but couldn't quite.

"I'll take you home, Mrs. Niles," the Englishman said. "Where do you live?"

"Just up the road." I felt myself on the verge of tears now that people were bothering about me again. I find it much easier to be brave when I haven't anybody to depend on.

I looked up at him and found him eyeing my costume quizzically.

"If you came in that, I fancy I can go in this—what?" he asked with a grin.

I nodded. "It isn't far," I said, "and it's still dark."

As we went out I heard them open the door to the library. A little sick wave went over me. Colonel Arbuthnot-Howe took my arm and led me down the path. The gate was open, so we got out without waking Tim. His lodge was dark, which struck me as queer even then. I figured later that Thorn and I had left the side gate open when we came in. I couldn't remember having closed it.

York Road was perfectly silent as we went along it. The college campus was dark, except for the dim fan light in the President's House. We didn't say anything until we came to the corner of King Charles Street.

"This is where I live," I said then.

"Have you got a key?"

I shook my head. "We never lock our doors in Landover."

"You'd better to-night." He said it so seriously that I was startled.

"Why?" I asked.

"Haven't you seen enough for one night?"

"Plenty," I said.

"Good night, Mrs. Niles."

He took my hand in both of his and looked gravely down at my upturned face.

"Will you tell me all about this to-morrow?" he asked gently; and I'm rather ashamed to admit that my heart gave a perfectly shameless flutter and turned completely over.

"If you wish. Thanks for bringing me home. Good night."

I went to bed, but I couldn't go to sleep. The moment I

was alone with my eyes closed, the ghastly picture of Mr. Sutton dead, his head with that gaping wound, lolled to one side against the wing smeared with blood, came back to me with horrible clarity. I drew my hand that had touched that terrible stain towards me.

I don't know why the idea that Mr. Sutton had been murdered in cold blood was so long in seeming horrible to me. I knew he was dead—that he'd been shot; and I must have known it wasn't suicide. Dan recognized it as murder. I knew that. Yet the actual fact of murder *by* someone, someone I knew, probably, didn't seem important until I closed my eyes and tried to go to sleep. Someone had shot Mr. Sutton. Someone who wanted him dead had deliberately killed him!

My mind was so numb with weariness that even then it all seemed very remote. I don't think I doubted that when I got up in the morning and went down York Road to Seaton Hall, Mr. Sutton would be at the lodge talking to Tim Healy. It was the same illusion that one has in seeing Walter Hampden die as Hamlet one night and walk the boards as Othello the next. I'm afraid I'm never quite sure what's real and what isn't.

I tried to think over the steps in the swift events of that day. It was hazy then. Now it's all very clear.

It began when I saw Sebastien Baca sitting on my brick wall. Surely, I thought, that was longer ago than just this very morning—yesterday morning, now? It seemed years ago that I saw him catch the falling magnolia petal, and sat across from him at lunch. His account of the Ranch of the Spring of the Holy Ghost was as remote now as the actual ranch had been when he described it to us.

Then there was Reverdy's visit to Mr. Sutton, and my visit to Aunt Charlotte and meeting with Mr. Sutton there. Then Colonel Arbuthnot-Howe's arrival from Washington with Wally Fenton. Next dinner, and our bathing party that so nearly ended Mr. Baca. Through all of it ran the thread of Thorn's quarrel with her uncle, and her curious conduct that night; Wally's face with terror on it, Mr. Sutton's with death on it.

I went to sleep, and I didn't wake up until Lillie brought my breakfast and told me the devil had got Mr. Sutton and I needn't say he hadn't. Also Jack said some one had taken his flashlight from the hall closet and did I know where it was.

XIII

All the incredible business of the night came back. Mr. Sutton was dead. I poured a cup of coffee and stirred it slowly, thinking. My coat was lying half on a chair and half on the floor where I'd thrown it. My tennis slippers were beside it. I thought of the slip of paper in my pocket, but I found in myself a curious reluctance now to look at it.

Ben came in, on his way to class.

"Lillie tells me Mr. Sutton was shot last night," he said, kissing my forehead absently.

I nodded. "How did she know, do you think?"

"How do they know everything that happens anywhere in town," he replied. "Is that clock right?"

"A little fast. It's too bad about Mr. Sutton."

He sat down on the foot of my bed and regarded me with a sort of affectionate disinterest.

"You liked him, didn't you, Martha," he said after a moment, as if he were stating a curious but true proposition.

I nodded.

"I never could understand it," he went on. "I've tried to follow you, but you like such odd people. I've about given it up. I don't really care, as long as you don't stop liking me."

I reassured him.

"Didn't you ever like him at all?" I asked.

"He was so grossly immoral. Oh, I don't mean in the ordinary sense. I mean in his human relationships."

"Because he was disgustingly rich?"

"Not at all, though I think what he did with his money is evidence of my point. He never gave it away except where it brought him the greatest prestige. I mean he never had anything but a purely selfish and egotistical motive in any of his gifts. Barton at the Polytechnic told me they rued the day he'd ever given them a dime."

"But he could be kind," I protested mildly, knowing how true anything anyone wanted to say against Mr. Sutton was.

"And often was, until somebody crossed him. That case of Dan, for instance."

Dan Sutton was engaged to Joan Frazier, the daughter of one of our science professors at Landover, and Mr. Sutton managed it so that the man lost his job. He sent Dan to Europe for a year and when he got back the Fraziers had

61

disappeared. I don't think Mr. Sutton had anything against Joan Frazier—or in the present instance—against Franklin Knox. He simply seemed bent on not having his children marry.

"I didn't think you'd remember that," I remarked.

"As I remember, it was all I heard breakfast, lunch and dinner for a year," Ben said maliciously. "As a matter of fact, I had forgotten it until last week. I forgot to tell you I saw Frazier at the University Club in Baltimore. He said Joan had a job in New York on a magazine or something. Dan was with me."

This, and coming from my husband, was a greater shock than any I'd got so far. I stared at him in amazement.

"Well, I've got to shove along," he said, with a glance at his watch. "Don't get too upset about this, will you, old girl? Just remember murder's one of the oldest of the arts. So long."

He went as far as the door and stopped with a puzzled frown on his face. My gaze followed his to my tweed coat tumbled half on and half off the chair, and then to my tennis slippers.

"You were out last night?" he said.

I nodded.

"By the way," he went on; "do you happen to know who shot Sutton?"

I shook my head. He shrugged his shoulders, got out his pipe, stepped closer to the fireplace and knocked the ashes out—which is something I've tried to make him stop doing, along with leaving the soap in his shaving brush, for ten years.

"The unfortunate part of this sort of thing," he said, "of course is that somebody has to do it. I mean if a man like Sutton could be done away with without the stigma of murder attaching to any other individual, there'd be something to be said for it. Well, I've got to get on. I'm lecturing on murder in primitive society this morning. Convenient, isn't it?"

"So that's it," I said. "I thought you were actually interested in Mr. Sutton. I was getting alarmed."

His smiling reply was drowned in the quick jangle of the telephone on my table.

"Hello. Yes, Dan. All right. As soon as I can."

Mr. Sullivan was to be at Seaton Hall at 9:30 and wanted me to come over.

Ben smiled. "Poor Martha," he said ironically. "You're going to have a lovely time. Don't forget to tell Lillie about lunch."

"If you promise not to forget to come home and eat it."

"I only forget to come home when there's chipped beef in library paste and baked apple."

I wish I could achieve Ben's pleasant detachment from everyday affairs.

The idea that someone was responsible for Mr. Sutton's death from an academic point of view was one thing. Stated in another way, that someone, almost certainly someone I knew, had confronted Mr. Sutton in his library, with a gun in his hand and murder in his heart and had shot him dead, it was something very different. I don't think that even then I was aware of the full meaning of what Ben had said about the stigma of murder. I began to be very shortly, however. Between the time I went into the bathroom to take a shower and the time I told Lillie what to order for lunch and got my hat, the telephone rang fourteen times.

Mrs. Robbins wanted to know if I'd heard about Mr. Sutton. Professor Robbins—he teaches Browning, Fielding, Thackeray and the Manly Authors generally—thought probably it was one of the tramps they'd seen on the railroad tracks. I said possibly, knowing Mrs. Robbins thought probably it was Miss Carter herself who'd done it, and hoped I thought so too.

Mrs. Weeks called up about the Woman's Club concert and said by the way wasn't it awful about Mr. Sutton. I agreed and hung up rather sharply.

Miss Taney called up to see if Jack could come over and play with Bobbie and wasn't it the strangest thing about Mr. Sutton. And so on, until my telephone manner, never very suave, became positively offensive.

I got down to Seaton Hall at half-past nine. A small knot of town loafers, white of course because when there's trouble the colored people stay as far away from it as they can, had gathered in York Road. They usually hang around the county courthouse in the Circle, but a little excitement draws them like flies. "Rich," one of the colored gardeners, had taken Tim's place at the gate, which he unbarred as I came up.

I missed old Tim. This seemed the time of all others when he should have been at his post to give the blessing of God's angels.

"Where's Mr. Healy, Rich?" I asked.

He shrugged his lanky shoulders.

" 'Deed an' Ah don' know, Miss."

He closed the gate in the face of the village loafers with considerable pleasure, I thought.

Jim Basil, the state policeman, was at the door when I

went in, trim in his olive drab and awfully decent. His father owns the electrical shop. It was something, I thought, not to have one of Landover's shuffling old hacks in his baggy blue, spitting tobacco juice into the laurel bushes and azaleas.

"Good morning, Mrs. Niles," he said. "Mr. Sullivan's inside. I think they're expecting you."

Inside there were a few people I didn't know and a snappy young man with a broken-out face, and a horribly antiseptic smell of Lifebuoy Soap and Listerine that I did.

"This way, Mrs. Niles. Mr. Sullivan is waiting."

I dislike important young men, but there didn't seem any adequate way of indicating the fact sufficiently to make it apparent to him. So I went on into the front drawing room, where Mr. Sullivan was sitting behind a bridge table writing. He was alone.

"Hello," I said and sat down.

He smiled at me. "You don't look as though you'd been roaming around the country until four o'clock in the morning, Mrs. Niles," he said pleasantly.

"Was I?" I asked in surprise.

"Weren't you? Young Sutton says you left here at quarter to four."

"I suppose that's right. I hadn't thought of the time very much."

"And that's just what you've got to do, Mrs. Niles," he said very seriously, fixing me with his colorless eyes glinting under beetling eyebrows. I recognized the look. It's the professional cross-examining look, most successful on scared country folk and trembling Negroes.

"Don't you try to frighten me, Mr. Sullivan," I said. "Now that you remind me of it, I haven't had much sleep, and there's no use of our having a quarrel."

He moved his papers about in front of him with a smile.

"Very well, Mrs. Niles; but I'm quite serious about this. Now, as far as I can make out, you were in and out of here all day, yesterday."

"And far into the night," I added, with a slight attempt at irony.

"So it would seem."

And then he did a strange thing. He leaned across the bridge table, tapping his papers with the rubber end of his pencil. He fixed me again with professionally narrowed eye.

"Mrs. Niles, you have the key to this whole affair. And I've got to get it from you; do you understand?"

I sat back in my chair and stared at him in open amazement. As our eyes met it occurred to me even more sharply

64

that I was now talking to the State's Attorney, not to the Mr. Sullivan I talked to on the street corner every afternoon.

He got up and came around the table, and stood in front of me.

"Look here, Mrs. Niles. Daniel Sutton has been murdered, murdered, mark you me; and it's my duty to find out who murdered him, and send him to the gallows. Do you understand that, Mrs. Niles?"

He turned on his heel and went back to his chair. I was left most completely dumfounded. I began to wonder if Mr. Sullivan thought I had murdered Daniel Sutton.

"Now," he said, smiling grimly, "what can you tell me?"

"What do you want me to say, Mr. Sullivan?"

"I want you to tell me what frightened you when you stood in that room, before you saw Daniel Sutton's dead body. When I know that, Mrs. Niles, I expect to know what it was that Tim Healy saw through the library window—what it was that shocked Tim Healy to death. Literally, Mrs. Niles, mark you me, shocked him to death."

"Tim Healy? Dead?"

"Dead. Tim Healy, dead!"

The State's Attorney repeated my horrified whisper in sharp staccato.

XIV

So I got two profound shocks within five minutes of entering Seaton Hall; and of the two, I think Mr. Sullivan's manner was almost the more profound. I'm afraid I always assume that everybody else has the same background and plays by the same set of conventions that I do. It was a serious blow to me when I discovered that my hairdresser honestly couldn't see why her baby shouldn't use a teething ring. She looks more intelligent than most women I know. The fact that my butcher is head of the local Klan and has an extraordinarily deep-seated conviction that Catholics and Jews are a menace absolutely astounds me. So when Mr. Sullivan, whom I'd assumed was equipped with exactly the same prejudices that Ben has, and I have, and Thorn Carter has, and Dr. Knox has, turned out not to be at all, I was amazed.

It seemed, in short, that Mr. Sullivan was just what a sensible person would assume he was—a small town prosecuting attorney who'd played the local political game for thirty years. He was like the other people that sit in on the game. As my husband explained patiently to me at dinner that night, he was eminently fitted to deal with the people he normally has to deal with. Most of our crime—which is very little—is committed by Negroes and low-grade whites. It shouldn't have been surprising, then, that when Mr. Sullivan was confronted with murder at Seaton Hall, he reacted to the fact of murder and not to the fact of Seaton Hall.

I'm convinced, in looking back on all this, that if he had used different tactics with me, things would not have ended as they did. Heaven knows I had left home and walked down York Road past the knot of village idiots and into Seaton Hall with the best will in the world. It seems to me that I just took it for granted that the person who murdered Daniel Sutton would be found and punished. I didn't even have Ben's attitude that whoever he was he had done a public service. I hadn't, as far as I know, the least intention of not telling Mr. Sullivan, or somebody, everything I knew; it simply hadn't occurred to me to do anything else.

But when he began flashing the witness stand pyrotechnic at me, I discovered to my amazement that he was putting me in the curious position of third conspirator, and I simply went into my shell like a snail whose nose is being poked with a straw, if snails have noses. It wasn't entirely his manner. You expect prosecuting attorneys to fix you with penetrating glances and that sort of thing. But his attitude was so exactly that I had come there with every intention of preventing him from doing his duty, and that I'd mighty soon see that the majesty of the law brooked no interference from anybody.

For that reason, I suppose, I kept my mouth as shut as possible, when he first horrified me with his cruel announcement of poor Tim's death, and then told me that I was the key to the whole thing.

"Mrs. Niles," he said, still tapping the table with his pencil, "what time did you leave this house last night?"

"Just before one. And again just before four."

"What were you doing here each time?"

"We were here to dinner and stayed late. I came back after we'd gone because Thorn Carter came after me."

I suppose I ought to have suspected something when he let that pass.

"Professor Niles was with you?"

"Mr. Niles was with me the first time."

"But not the second."

"No."

66

"Were you alone the second time, that is at four o'clock this morning?"

"I came with Thorn Carter and Colonel Arbuthnot-Howe took me home."

"You say that Miss Thorn Carter came for you. When was that?"

"About half-past two."

"Where were you?"

"I was in bed."

"You came directly back here with her?"

"No, we sat and talked for a while."

"Before you came back here."

"Yes."

"Mrs. Niles, why did Miss Carter come after you?"

"Mr. Sullivan, she wasn't feeling very well and she was rather troubled, I think. In fact she heard someone in the hall, and I understand that she ran out of the house and down to my place without thinking a lot about it."

"Mrs. Niles, when you and Miss Thorn came back, how did you get in?"

"What do you mean?"

"Which way did you come in?"

"Through the gate."

"On York Road?"

I nodded.

"Mrs. Niles, you know this house very well, don't you?"

"Pretty well."

"Isn't it the custom here to keep that gate locked?"

"Surely."

"What time was it when you and Miss Thorn came back here?"

"Around three o'clock."

"Do you remember if the gate was locked, or not?"

"It was locked."

"Mrs. Niles, who let you in?"

I looked at him in surprise.

"I suppose it was Tim, though we didn't see him. He clicked the latch to let us in."

He looked at me strangely.

"You're sure of that?"

"Yes."

"And Miss Thorn was with you?"

"Certainly."

"And it was about three o'clock."

"Yes. I'm quite sure of that because the clock struck three

67

a very few minutes later when Thorn and I were going up stairs."

He wrote something on a piece of paper and studied it thoughtfully.

"Mrs. Niles, when you came in the house who let you in?"

"We walked in. The front door was open."

"Was there a light in the hall?"

"Yes, a dim one."

"What did you do, Mrs. Niles, when you came in?"

I figured a few seconds too without the aid of a piece of paper or pencil.

"We came in," I said at last. "We heard Mr. Sutton moving about in the library. The door was slightly ajar. I could just see there was a light in there."

"Just a moment. Had you seen that light when you came up the drive? The library corresponds to this room, does it not, with two long windows opening on little balconies on the York Road side?"

"Yes."

"Then didn't you see the light as you came up the drive?"

"No, I didn't. You know how heavy these hangings are."

I pointed to the gold damask at the drawing room windows.

"In the library the drapes are heavy lined velvet, and Mr. Sutton not only has them drawn at night but the inside shutters closed too. If the room was lighted with thousand candle power lamps you wouldn't see it from outside."

Mr. Sullivan wrote again. Then he polished his spectacles deliberately with a big green handkerchief.

"And you saw no light from the outside."

"No."

"Go on, please."

"Where was I?"

"You came in the hall and saw a light in the library."

"We heard Mr. Sutton moving about. I suggested to Thorn that she say good night to him, or something."

"Did she?"

"She didn't care to disturb him. I suppose if a man stays up until three he has some reason for it and wouldn't care to be disturbed."

"Was that the reason Miss Thorn gave?"

"I don't think she gave any reason. She was tired and I suggested she go to bed."

"Why did you also suggest she go in and see him?"

"No particular reason."

68

"Mrs. Niles, she came to you very much disturbed about something, did she not?"

I nodded.

"And you were sufficiently concerned to come back here with her at three o'clock in the morning."

"It wasn't that particularly. She was uneasy and didn't care to come back alone."

"And didn't care to say good night to her uncle in that room over across the hall?"

Mr. Sullivan leaned forward. I caught the District Attorney's gaze again.

"No, apparently she didn't."

"And you didn't care to go in."

"My dear Mr. Sullivan, why should I? I had on a tweed coat over my night dress, a pair of tennis shoes on, and my nose wasn't powdered. I not only didn't care to go in to see Mr. Sutton, I positively wanted not to see him."

"Yet you did go in—didn't you?"

I looked up in surprise.

"You did go in the library, only half an hour later, didn't you?"

"Yes. But I didn't go in to see Mr. Sutton. I was coming down the stairs. I heard somebody or something in the back drawing room, and I was frightened. I knew Mr. Sutton was in the library because we'd heard him, and my first impulse was to get to somebody at once."

"Why didn't you go back upstairs?"

"It was easier to go down. Thorn was the only person awake upstairs anyway. I suppose I felt that a man would be safer to be with."

"In other words, you weren't concerned about your clothes at that time."

"Good Lord, no. I'd completely forgotten them."

He nodded sagely, and to my intense annoyance wrote something down.

"Mrs. Niles, when you got down, was the library door open?"

"No, it was closed."

"When was it closed?"

"Obviously some time within the half hour I was upstairs with Thorn Carter."

Mr. Sullivan gazed absently out of the window for a moment.

"Mrs. Niles, what sort of a noise was it you heard from the stairway?"

"It was somebody moving very cautiously, I thought towards the hall where I was. At least it seemed to come closer while I stood there."

"You know the house very well, don't you, Mrs. Niles?"

I agreed again that I knew the house. He apparently thought better of the question he was going to ask, for quite suddenly he changed his manner to a neighborly confidential one, which, I may say, didn't in the least deceive me.

"Mrs. Niles, do you know anyone who would want Mr. Sutton out of the way?"

"I know just the same number that you do, Mr. Sullivan," I replied affably. I remembered a conversation that he and I had had last Christmas at an egg-nogg party at the Tavenners, in which he said that if Daniel Sutton were found dead some frosty morning they could hang everybody in town and not be far wrong. And Mr. Sullivan remembered it too, and smiled a little in answer to my smile. But he recovered himself quickly.

"Seriously, Mrs. Niles. You know these people better than I do; but I know at least three people who have possible motive. You know more than that."

I shook my head.

"Mrs. Niles, I'll put my cards on the table." That's a favorite Landover cliché. In a few minutes he'd have his shoulder to the wheel and his nose to the grindstone.

"There's Reverdy Hawkins's crowd who thought they had their hands on real money. There's young Dan—I suppose you know Joan Frazier's back in town?"

I didn't, but I nodded my head.

"Then there's young Knox and Miss Thorn Carter."

I looked up inquiringly.

"You know what I mean, Mrs. Stiles. My wife told me yesterday that Sutton had threatened to disinherit his niece if she saw young Knox again. Last night Terry saw young Knox go in the side door of the President's House at two o'clock."

Terry is the college watchman.

"You're wrong about Thorn and Franklin, Mr. Sullivan," I said. "You ought to know that town gossip isn't reliable, especially about the people here at Seaton Hall. Mr. Sutton didn't want Thorn to marry Franklin; that's all. He didn't forbid her to see him again. Anyway, if Franklin went in his house at two o'clock, that would seem to let him out, wouldn't it? Tim let us in here at three, and we heard Mr. Sutton in the library."

Again the strange glance that I had noticed before.

70

"Mrs. Niles, did you hear the shot that killed Mr. Sutton while you were upstairs?"

"No, I didn't."

"No, Mrs. Niles," he repeated, with heavy emphasis. "You didn't hear it—for the very adequate reason that Sutton was shot at half-past one. And Tim Healy died at half-past one, Mrs. Niles. Tim Healy didn't let you in that gate. You didn't hear Mr. Sutton moving about in the library. When you came in through the front door into the hall, at three o'clock, Tim Healy was lying in the laurel bushes under the library windows, and Daniel Sutton was sitting in the library in the wing chair. And they were both dead, Mrs. Niles."

XV

Mr. Sullivan gave me time to take that in. More time, in fact, than I needed. It struck me as being ludicrously like a caption on the screen—you have time to read it and forget it a dozen times before the film goes on. I suppose that like the movies Mr. Sullivan was designed for people who don't get things very quickly. Perhaps he was waiting for me to commit myself in some way. When I said nothing he got up and came around the table in front of me.

"Mrs. Niles! *What* did you hear in the library?"

"I don't know," I said. "I thought it was Mr. Sutton."

"And who let you and Thorn Carter in the gate?"

"I don't know. I thought it was Tim Healy."

"Mrs. Niles," he began again. I writhed at last at the terrible repetition of my name. I think he saw he was annoying me, for he stopped and began again.

"Mrs. Niles, are you sure you and Miss Thorn did not look in the library?"

"Positive," I replied.

"Now then. You heard the buzz of the telephone. And you suggested to Miss Thorn that she go in and say good night to her uncle."

"I did."

Mr. Sullivan began a slow pacing up and down in front of me, hands clasped behind his back.

"Mrs. Niles, think this over carefully. How did you know it was the telephone in the library that you heard?"

"Because I've heard it a thousand times. It's a direct inner connection between the library and the lodge and the serv-

71

ants' pantry, put there so that Tim could announce visitors either to Mr. Sutton or to Lafayette. But I'd never heard it late at night, and that's why I didn't recognize it as the lodge phone, I suppose."

"But Miss Thorn did?"

"Naturally."

"Mrs. Niles, when Miss Thorn said she didn't care to see her uncle, you weren't surprised?"

"Not in the least."

"Doesn't it seem to you now that Miss Thorn may have had a reason for *not* wishing to see her uncle?"

"I suppose she did have a reason for it."

He smiled grimly.

"What do you suppose it was?"

"Simply that no one, to my knowledge, ever intruded on Mr. Sutton when he was in the library, without being sent for. Then in the second place Thorn and her uncle had . . ."

Mr. Sullivan caught me up almost before I had realized that I was going too far.

"Yes, Mrs. Niles. Miss Thorn and her uncle had quarreled before she left the house. Now then: doesn't it occur to you that one of the reasons Miss Thorn didn't want to go in that library was that she knew, *at that time*, mark you me, Mrs. Niles, that her uncle was dead?"

I don't think that Mr. Sullivan realized how keenly I felt a sudden sick feeling inside of me.

"Not in a thousand years," I said.

He shrugged his shoulders, went back behind the table and sat down, looking reflectively at me.

Finally he got up and put a book on his papers.

"Mrs. Niles, I want you to come with me, if you don't mind, and show me just where you stood when you heard what you thought was Mr. Sutton in the library."

I did mind intensely. But I said "Certainly," and followed him out into the hall.

His objectionable assistant was still talking there to Matthew and Colonel Arbuthnot-Howe. The Englishman shot me an encouraging but I thought also slightly derisive smile. Mr. Sullivan, ignoring all of them in a matter-of-fact way, proceeded to the front door and turned around, with a glance at me.

"We came in here and stopped," I said. "It was perfectly still. Then we heard someone move about. We realized that it was Mr. Sutton and came on into the hall until we got about here where we could see that door."

I pointed to the library door, open a little.

72

"We couldn't see it from back there, if you'll notice, because it's set back in the thick wall."

"How much open was it, Mrs. Niles."

"About six inches."

"All right. Now then, Mrs. Niles, go up the stairs and stop where you did when you came down."

I went up about eight steps and turned around.

"I was about here. I had my right hand on the bannister like this. I could see the drawing room door here, open, and I'd already seen from upstairs that the library door had been closed."

"You hadn't heard anyone come up?"

"No."

"Did it occur to you, Mrs. Niles, that the person you heard in the parlor here was the person you'd heard in the library?"

"No, it didn't."

"Go on, Mrs. Niles."

"All of a sudden I got panicky, but I couldn't call out or . . . do anything. So I suppose I just made a dash for the library where Mr. Sutton was. When I opened the door it was dark. It seemed ages before I got to the switch and turned on the lights. I turned around facing the hall, and I must have just stood there waiting for something to come, until I . . . my hand . . . touched Mr. Sutton."

Mr. Sullivan nodded his comprehension.

"Would you mind coming into the library, Mrs. Niles?"

I didn't want to go in the library; in fact I definitely wanted not to go in. I happened to look at Colonel Arbuthnot-Howe. He shook his head.

"Do you mind if I come along?" he said to Mr. Sullivan, with an encouraging glance at me.

Mr. Sullivan agreed promptly. The more the merrier seemed to be the idea. Of course there wasn't any very good reason for my not wanting to go in the library. I'd been in it thousands of times before last night. And I found when I stepped over the threshold that the night before already seemed very unreal. It was like something I'd seen in a dream, and only vaguely remembered as a dream. But Mr. Sullivan saw to it that that didn't last long.

"You were standing here?"

He pointed to the spot where I had stood behind the high back of the Chippendale wing chair. I nodded.

"What did you see?"

"I didn't see anything, until my hand slipped down the wing here. I was watching the hall."

Mr. Sullivan turned to Colonel Arbuthnot-Howe.

"You were the first in the room, I understand."

The Englishman nodded gravely.

"What did *you* see?"

He smiled a little grimly.

"I saw Mrs. Niles's hand with blood on it, and I saw Mr. Sutton with a bullet wound in his head. I didn't see a gun. I looked for one at once, that is as soon as I got Mrs. Niles to a chair. I saw the window at the side open a little. The safe in the corner was also standing open. Otherwise there was no disorder in the room."

I looked around first at the safe, then at the window, then back at the two men who were watching me with very different expressions. Mr. Sullivan it seemed had scored a minor triumph, and was not a little pleased with it. But Colonel Arbuthnot-Howe came to my rescue.

"It's perfectly natural, of course, Mr. Sullivan," he said, lighting a cigarette and putting the burnt match carefully back in the box, "that Mrs. Niles should not see any of those things. She was expecting to see something in the hall, and when she quite accidentally was forced to look at Mr. Sutton she was too shocked to notice anything else. I noticed her particularly later when the others came. She was sitting in that chair, still looking towards the hall. She glanced at the two young Suttons when they came in, and at Miss Atwood when she stood in the hall. At no time did she look towards the safe or the window."

Mr. Sullivan pursed his lips.

"I should say," the Englishman went on, "that it would have been rather surprising under the circumstances if Mrs. Niles had seen the room in detail."

"You did, of course," I said. I was a little annoyed by the assumption that you can't expect intelligent conduct from women in an emergency.

He smiled.

"I've had experience enough to know what to look for."

"There's one other thing, Mrs. Niles," said Mr. Sullivan. "Will you step over here to the window, please."

The library at Seaton Hall is a long room, half the length of the house, with two long windows in front and one at the side. The elaborately carved fireplace is on the right side next to the hall. It is flanked by two doors, one of which is blind, the other the one we saw ajar the night before. The side windows open out onto a little balcony, and overlook the small brick-paved area in front of the hyphen that connects the kitchen wing to the house. The dining room is directly back of the library and opens into the hyphen, where the

74

pantries are. There is therefore only one door into the library. The front windows are always locked, and in the evening tightly shuttered.

It is a beautiful room. The walls are completely lined with books except on the sides of the fireplace. Here there are several portraits of old-fashioned gentlemen that Mr. Sutton bought at Christie's. In the center of the room is a long table, and at the end nearest the windows is another table at right angles to it. This is Mr. Sutton's work table. His secretary has a desk between the windows.

I followed Mr. Sullivan between the desk and the table to the window. It was still open. He stepped aside and I looked out. In the broken crushed laurel bushes below I read the fall of Tim Healy. Poor good Tim Healy.

"Do you think Tim shot him?" I asked before I knew what I was saying.

"He was shot from a close range, Mrs. Niles. Probably not more than three feet."

"Then what about Tim?"

"Tim died of heart failure. Dr. McPherson has treated him for five years. There's no doubt of that, he died of pure shock."

Mr. Sullivan led the way back towards the hall. He looked tired and not nearly as sure of himself.

"I figure that this is what happened, Mrs. Niles," he said. "For some reason Healy came up this way around half-past one. Maybe he saw the light you and Miss Thorn Carter didn't see. He came to see what was the matter. It would seem that he suspected something wrong, since he. didn't come through the front door. And just as he looked in, before he could speak, he saw someone he knew shoot Mr. Sutton dead. You could still read the surprise and the horror on the face when I saw him. He staggered backwards and fell; his heart stopped beating."

The French clock on the mantel ticked hastily along towards eleven o'clock in the dead silence of the room. Mr. Sullivan continued.

"Tim's watch struck the railing of the basement window when he fell, and broke, and the hands stopped at 1.32. The window was open when I came at ten minutes after four. Now, Mrs. Niles, I want you to think again whether or not you saw a light in this room."

"I positively did not," I replied quietly.

"Then that's all this morning, Mrs. Niles. The photographers have been here from Baltimore and they've taken the finger prints on the telephone. We'll know this evening who called from the lodge and who answered here."

I started to go.

"I'll trouble you to make your finger prints on the card here, please, Mrs. Niles."

I took off my gloves and went through with it.

"Thank you, Mrs. Niles."

"You're quite welcome, Mr. Sullivan."

I went out into the hall. Colonel Arbuthnot-Howe followed me, and together, and without a word, we went out the garden end of the hall and sat down on the verandah. I was a rag. I took one of the cigarettes he handed me and waited until he lighted it. Then I drew a tremendous sigh of relief.

He sat down and crossed his legs, regarding me calmly, with his quizzical little smile that wrinkled up his steely blue eyes in a very engaging and very disarming fashion. After a moment he leaned forward and flicked the ash from his cigarette.

"Mrs. Niles," he began.

"If I am called Mrs. Niles once more today," I said viciously, "I'll commit worse than murder."

He grinned broadly.

"Very well—Martha," he said, and I blushed unnecessarily.

XVI

"Are you busy, Colonel Arbuthnot-Howe?" I asked. "If you aren't let's stroll down towards the water. I'd like some sound advice."

"That's very flattering," he said, getting to his feet. We went down the terrace steps.

I felt he was naturally waiting for me to begin, but I didn't. In the first place I wasn't quite sure what I wanted to ask him. If Mr. Sullivan had set out to make me nervous about Thorn and my little expedition of the night before, he had succeeded very effectively. I was beginning to see what a difficult position Thorn had got herself into. And that is a queer thing about social psychology. There's no doubt that at this moment I was ready to do anything to save Thorn from Mr. Sullivan's code of laws, innocent or guilty. In fact, I suspect that the question of guilt was the one furthest from my mind. My entire problem was how to circumvent Mr. Sullivan.

76

There was another reason for my not beginning until we'd got out of the long avenue of terraced lawn stretching from the porch to the water.

"The house makes a perfect sounding board," I explained softly to my companion. "On the porch you can hear everything that's even whispered down here."

"So I've learned," he said. I looked at him in surprise. "How did you learn it?"

"Last night a number of people were walking up and down out here while I was on the porch," he answered casually; and added, lowering his voice, although we were now out of earshot, "Among other things I heard Fenton tell Baca that Mr. Sutton was changing his will to-day, disinheriting Thorn Carter, who, it seems, is determined to marry a young fellow named Knox."

"Oh dear," I said unhappily.

"My dear Mrs. Niles—sorry!—that sort of thing is bound to get out. There's no use in your trying to hide it from me or anybody else."

"Who do you think," I said point-blank, "Mr. Sullivan is after?"

"Offhand I'd say he thinks Miss Thorn Carter shot her uncle."

As the question of guilt was thus put directly up to me, I had to consider it.

"Do you think she shot him?" I asked.

He shrugged.

"I don't know. I don't know her well enough to say. Just the same I haven't a doubt that if she was sufficiently provoked she'd display . . . ah . . . considerable courage."

"Do you think it takes courage to shoot a man in cold blood?" I demanded warmly.

"Oh, rather," he said. Without waiting for my remonstrance he went on. "You see this morning Sullivan—not too intelligent, that fellow, if you ask me—questioned everybody and got them all placed. I mean when the shooting occurred, if and in so far as one knows when the shooting occurred. The placing begins at the point when we came up from the river."

"You and Susan and Wally and I walked up, didn't we." He nodded.

"And your husband and the secretary chap were playing chess in the drawing room. Mr. Sutton and Dr. Knox were in the library together, talking. Miss Carter had retired and the two Sutton boys and Miss Thorn were getting Baca to bed with mustard plasters and things."

77

"That's right," I said. "And you and Wally went in the back drawing room."

"Yes. And then Miss Atwood came in and broke up the chess; and before you people left Miss Thorn came down stairs."

"Awfully upset about something."

"Yes; or looking very determined at any rate."

I had a very clear picture of Thorn's white face and set jaw as she stood at the foot of the stairs saying good night to us.

"After you left Dan and Bill Sutton came down and said they'd got the doctor. Not long after that Sutton and Dr. Knox came out of the library. We all had a drink of some very good Bourbon and Dr. Knox went home. I talked to Mr. Sutton on the porch about half an hour, and we went in.

"He said he had some work he wanted to do. Then something happened that I thought was interesting—or that I now think may be interesting. Mr. Sutton told Dan that he'd telephoned to a Mr. Rand. Rand was coming down in the morning, and Dan was to see that somebody met him with a car in Baltimore. Dan said, 'What's he coming for?' Mr. Sutton said, 'I'm making some changes in my will.' "

We looked steadily at each other.

"Who was there when he said that?"

"The two young Suttons, Miss Atwood, Thorn Carter, and I. Lafayette—is that his name?—was there too. Fenton was about somewhere."

"Susan Atwood of course wasn't affected," I said. "She's Miss Carter's ward, and has money of her own besides."

"She's luckier than Miss Thorn."

I agreed.

"That brings us to a little after one. The clock struck as Mr. Sutton and I were coming in from the verandah. We stood about talking for a few minutes, until Miss Atwood announced that she was going to bed and went. The rest of us followed her up except Miss Thorn Carter. She said something to her uncle. He said, 'Come in the library then.' She followed him in and closed the door."

"That's about quarter past one," I said.

"About. Now then, so far we have witnesses to all that. We haven't witnesses, at least not human ones, for anything else. Have we?"

"Susan said she saw Mr. Baca from her window sometime after she went upstairs."

78

"At two o'clock, to be exact. Montezuma, as she calls him, hunting an empire of gold, probably."

"He'll hardly find it here."

"This is exactly where he will find it," remarked the Colonel easily.

"By the way," I said, "how does it happen that you aren't in the guest wing with Mr. Baca?"

"Mr. Bill Sutton is responsible for that. He gave me his room so he could keep an eye on Baca, if he needed anything nights."

"You're in Bill's room? But that's on the third floor."

"No. Fenton traded with me and moved up there. So I don't have to do so many steps. My leg got smashed up and I'm not so clever at steps. I was in Fenton's room."

"Oh," I said.

"So there you have everybody's word, and nothing else, for the rest of the night. Bill sleeping and taking care of Baca, who was presumed to be in bed. All the rest the same.

"Everybody," he added with an ironic smile, "carefully tucked away."

"Did you hear Thorn come upstairs?" I asked. "Your room is next to hers."

"I didn't hear her."

"Would you have heard her if she did come up?"

"Not necessarily. She hadn't dressed after they rescued Baca, if you remember. When she came downstairs she had on some sort of slippers. Anyway, those walls are thick, and so are the doors."

"So that Thorn may very easily have stayed down stairs, shot her uncle at half-past one, and waited until a little after two to come over to my house. That doesn't sound very probable, though, does it?"

"That's why I used the word 'courage,' Mrs. Niles," replied Colonel Arbuthnot-Howe evenly. "As a matter of fact," he went on quickly, "it doesn't necessarily follow that Mr. Sutton's death occurred precisely at 1.30 simply because Healy's watch is stopped at that time. It's only a logical inference."

"What do you mean?"

"Oh, the watch might have been slow. It might have run down two days ago. It might have run fifteen minutes after the smash and then stopped. Or, of course, the murderer could have noticed Healy, slipped out there, broken the watch and turned the hands back an hour or so. Or, for that matter, Healy could have had a heart attack at 1.30 without any direct cause. You'd be amazed how uncanny coincidences can be."

"I constantly am," I said. "But I can't see that any of them would help Thorn very much."

He didn't say anything for a minute. Then he said, "Do you shoot?"

"Tin cans when I was a child. Why?"

"Does Miss Thorn shoot?"

I suppose I hesitated.

"She does?"

"Until last year they always took a shooting box in Scotland every August," I admitted reluctantly.

"In that case, Mrs. Niles," he said gravely, "there is one thing that seems true. Mr. Sullivan isn't far off the track when he believes that Thorn had a definite reason for not going in the library."

"Why?"

"When you came into the hall, just before three o'clock, didn't you notice a peculiar odor there?"

I remembered smelling something and said so.

"But you didn't recognize it?"

"No."

"Well, I recognized it about three-quarters of an hour later, and Miss Carter, knowing firearms, would have done, too. It was cordite, Mrs. Niles. So I think we can be positive of the point that she knew a gun had been fired downstairs. If she knew who fired it, or whom it was fired at, is another matter. All I can assume is that she preferred not to investigate. Not much doubt about Sullivan's conclusion."

"Look here, Colonel," I said flatly. "I don't believe Thorn shot her uncle at 1.30 or any other time. She said she heard a sound, and got up to go down stairs to see what it was. Somebody was in the hall when she went down about two o'clock. She was frightened and made a dash for the garden door and ran out."

"Strange, wasn't it? It's much more reasonable to suppose that being downstairs she found her way upstairs blocked, and not wanting to be seen, went out the garden door. Or, more reasonably still, she had some reason for going out."

I looked at him for a minute.

"Do you really think Thorn shot her uncle?" I asked.

"No. I'm afraid I don't."

"Then if I tell you everything I know about all this, will you find out who killed him, and make Mr. Sullivan leave her alone?"

He looked at me for some time. Then he said, "You'll tell me everything you know, and help me if I need it?"

"Yes."

He held out his hand with a grin.

"That's a promise," he said. "And I'm going to ask you to do something right away. Will you do it?"

"Surely."

"All right. Have you seen Baca this morning?"

"No."

"Go and call on him, and find out for me just how sick he really is."

"All right," I said. "Reports to be sent to the British Embassy?"

He grinned again at that. "No, just bring it to me."

We walked back towards the house. When we came in sight of the porch I saw the imposing white-haired figure of Nathan Rand. He was in the doorway, talking to Mr. Sullivan and Dan.

"There's Mr. Rand," I said joyfully.

XVII

When I saw Nathan Rand my immediate reaction was that I hadn't seen Dr. Knox that morning. Which was a perfectly logical association of ideas for a professor's wife. Mr. Rand is the chief figure in the college—chief extra-curricular figure, perhaps I should say—and his visits to Landover are always in the College's interest.

It struck me just then that of all the people connected with Mr. Sutton, Dr. Knox and Mr. Rand would be the only ones to whom his death would be a matter of regret, even dismay. The point is that they had always expected, or at any rate had labored as if they always expected, that Mr. Sutton would some day be the angel of the College. I remembered then that every year we've been at Landover College Dr. Knox has said, This will be the year. This year Mr. Sutton is going to do something for the college. This year always had managed to pass with the gift of a couple of thousand dollars, new uniforms for the band or a new piano for the Student Union; and that was all.

Nevertheless—so optimistic are college boards, presidents and faculties—we tightened our belts so to speak and said *Next* year Mr. Sutton will give us a million dollars. But now Mr. Sutton was dead without doing anything at all.

That all this ran through my mind isn't surprising, because it meant a slight readjustment of my own plans. One of the reasons we were concerned with Mr. Sutton's interest in the college—if you can call anything so lukewarm interest—was that salaries would go up if the college got some money. And as I went up to the sitting room of the guest wing I was mentally discarding a boarding school for the children next year. I decided not to turn in the Ford for a new Ford, or spend the summer in England, and I threw out a few other pieces of visionary timber that had increasingly got in the attic of my castle in Spain as long as Mr. Sutton was alive. Not that I minded *very* much. I had always had my doubts about Mr. Sutton anyway, and in the second place discarding used dreams is something one gets used to after a while.

The guest wing at Seaton Hall has a big living room, a library and a billiard room on the first floor. On the second there are three bedrooms and baths, and two other bedrooms and baths in the up-stairs part of the hyphen. Just now they were replacing a section of the old brick that had started to sweat and only two rooms upstairs were in use. That I supposed was the reason Colonel Arbuthnot-Howe was staying in the main house while Bill occupied the other room next to Mr. Baca's.

Mr. Baca was sitting in a big chair in the living room, a paler olive than he'd been the day before.

"Come in," he said, with a painful sort of smile. "It's so nice of you to come and see me."

"How do you feel this morning?"

"Better," he replied with a deprecatory shrug. "A bit rocky —but better."

"You're lucky to be alive at all, I suppose."

I took one of the brown cigarettes he handed me and sat down.

"I am, indeed." He spoke more fervently than the mere preservation of one's life from drowning seems to demand. I suppose Mexicans take such things rather harder than we do.

"I regret so deeply Mr. Sutton's death," he said after a moment; and then, quite suddenly, he shrugged his shoulders elaborately, and with a mocking smile said, "I have such bad luck!"

"How so?" It was odd that when he got excited his faultlessly constructed sentences became jerky and inaccurate.

"Because I come all the way from Mexico to see Mr. Sutton. I lose a hundred dollars on a horse in Louisville, and I think I must go back. But no, I say that is not a bad omen, I must go ahead. So I come. I find Mr. Sutton, I arrange my affairs with him. Not on very good terms, but better than I would suppose possible once I see Mr. Sutton. We get all arranged for. And then . . . he dies. But I say, maybe I can do business with the son. I believe in threes. The horse, the water, Mr. Sutton; I feel my luck must turn."

It seemed a very callous attitude, somehow. He seemed so beastly concerned with his own life and so little with Mr. Sutton's death.

"Were you doing business with him?" I said, for the want of anything better to say at the moment.

"Yes, and I was happy with the outcome. First you see I wanted him to deed me the rancho for myself, and I would pay him one dollar an acre."

"You mean that ranch you were telling us about at lunch?"

"Yes. But later when I talked to him we decided to go in it together, which was much better. But now . . ."

He shrugged his shoulders eloquently. I said nothing.

"It is all to do over again. And my present regret is that I am so in the way at such a delicate time."

"Are you in the way?" I asked with a smile.

"They all tell me I am not. But with such a sad thing happening, I feel very much that I should go at once. So I shall go to-morrow, and stop at an hotel in Baltimore until it is over."

"I shouldn't worry about that," I said. "Mr. Sullivan will probably stop you if you start anyway, and I'm afraid he won't understand your reason."

He looked at me with a surprised widening of his brilliant black eyes.

"I don't understand, Mrs. Niles?"

"I mean that everybody who was here last night has to stay here until the police let them go."

I was trying to find an ash tray, and when I looked at him he was staring at me with the most ludicrously amazed face I've ever seen.

"What *is* the matter, Mr. Baca?" I asked.

I find myself inclined to be extremely matter-of-fact around people with expressive eyes and gestures, probably to cover up my own lack of histrionic skill.

"What is the matter indeed, Mrs. Niles," he said, with a growing excitement. "I do not understand. The *police?* Did not Mr. Sutton die of heart failure last night?"

It was my turn to be surprised, and excited, a little. We stared at each other in a rather bewildered fashion.

"No, he didn't," I said at last. "That was the watchman. Mr. Sutton was shot. Murdered."

I can't describe the expression on the Mexican's face.

Whatever else had happened, I was perfectly convinced that up to that second he did not know, and had not the remotest suspicion, that Mr. Sutton's death was anything but natural. But though I can't describe the expression on his face, or rather the expressions, for one followed another quickly, it was clear from them, I thought, that now that he did know Mr. Sutton was murdered it meant more to him than to anyone else I'd seen. I had apparently thrown that information against a large background, where a place, which I knew nothing about, was all ready for it to fit in.

After his first excited exclamation in Spanish, which I didn't understand, Mr. Baca sat for a moment perfectly silent and motionless. I thought I could read on his extraordinarily mobile face amazement, uneasiness, anger, shock, understanding, defiance. Suddenly he made an attempt to get up, and as suddenly relaxed back into cushions. I couldn't tell whether he was weak or had decided abruptly that his best course was to remain in his ivory tower.

"Who told you Mr. Sutton died of a heart attack?" I ventured.

"The butler. I must have misunderstood. He said the master was dead and something about healing and heart."

"That's fair enough," I remarked with a smile, knowing how hard it is to understand Lafayette even when you're used to him unless you know what he's talking about. And I got up to go.

"Well," I said, "I've got to get back. I'm glad you're better. Has Dr. McPherson been to see you?"

"Not this morning, thank you."

I heard some steps in the hyphen, and recognized Susan's high heels. She opened the door.

"He's sitting up!" she said. "Hello, Martha. Thorn's been asking for you."

"I'm just going to see her."

"Not now you can't. Dr. Mac's just given her something to make her sleep. She's absolutely shot."

We left Mr. Baca, passing the doctor on our way down the hall. Susan took hold of my arm.

"It's ghastly about Thorn, Martha," she whispered. "She's in a frightful mess. I don't know what's the matter with her."

"Has she seen Franklin?"

She shook her head.

"She hasn't seen anybody."

"You let me know when she wakes up."

"Okay."

There's an entrance from the hyphen of the guest wing to

the house through the back drawing room, but I went outside and around the way I'd come in. Colonel Arbuthnot-Howe was moving unconcernedly back and forth across the first terrace, smoking his pipe. He looked up as I came out and strolled over to meet me. There was an amused twinkle in his eye and I shook my head.

"He's not *very* sick," I said. "Or at least he wasn't ten minutes ago. Dr. Mac and I dare say Susan are there now."

"I may take either of the two implications?"

"Or find a third. By the way, Mr. Baca's main trouble, as far as I could see, seems to be a badly bruised face."

He looked inquiringly at me.

"Has he been fighting?"

"I don't know. I suppose he struck a pile out in the channel that knocked him out. A girl last year did something of the kind."

Colonel Arbuthnot-Howe did not seem particularly impressed by my explanation, although he didn't say anything against it. I was just on the point of telling him about what Baca said about the ranch when Mr. Rand appeared on the verandah.

"Hello, Mrs. Niles!" he boomed. "Come in here—I want to talk to you."

XVIII

Mr. Rand is not an ordinary man. He's sort of a presence. His white leonine head, white mustache and Van Dyke, his twinkling merry blue eyes, his glasses hanging from his lapel on a black ribbon, his cavernous chuckle, his great bulk—everything about him is kindly and impressive. They say he is one of the most astute conference lawyers in New York.

"Hello!" I said, shaking hands with him. "It's nice to see you again. This is Colonel Arbuthnot-Howe. Mr. Rand."

They shook hands, both striking figures. They're about the same height, but Mr. Rand has considerable advantage in girth.

"I know Evelyn Arbuthnot-Howe in Surrey. Is there a connection?" asked Mr. Rand with his grave courtesy.

"Rather. He's my uncle. Many a drubbing he's given me. I spent most of an unfortunate youth at Esher."

"Ah, splendid. We must get together on this. You'll excuse us now?—I've got to talk to this young woman."

"Certainly, sir."

"Let's go in here, Mrs. Niles."

In the hall Mr. Sullivan's young man was firing questions at Lafayette in a ludicrous imitation of his senior's prosecuting manner. He quite subsided when he saw Mr. Rand, and Lafayette was quick to notice the change. The young man was in awe of Mr. Rand; Lafayette had known Mr. Rand when he was an undergraduate in Landover College. Therefore Lafayette was no longer in awe of the young man, and would never be again.

He stood aside and bowed amiably as we went into the drawing room, where Mr. Sullivan's papers were still spread out on the bridge table.

I had never seen Mr. Rand when he was engaged in anything more impressive than drinking one of Lafayette's mint juleps, or giving sheepskins—reluctantly paid for—to newly hatched bachelors of arts. I'll admit I stood—or sat now—in some awe of him myself. His twinkling eyes were troubled, his usually jovial face grave. I had the uncomfortable feeling that I'd done something I shouldn't have done, and that Jove was about to loose a mild but still devastating thunderbolt at my unworthy head.

"What's this all about, now, Mrs. Niles," he asked, drawing a chair close to mine and sitting down. "Sullivan tells me you found him."

I told him about it. He made a sympathetic clucking sound and shook his head. After all he is preeminently a gentleman of the old school; the idea of a lady's touching the cold murdered body of a friend was not pleasant or proper. In spite of his feeling Mr. Rand gave one the impression that he avoided unpleasant things. Perhaps unpleasant things avoided Mr. Rand.

"I got a call from Sutton about half-past seven last night," he said after a moment. "He said he had something important to talk to me about. He wanted me to come down. I'm pretty busy, but there's a board meeting at the college day after tomorrow and I decided I'd pack up and come for a few days with Sutton and Knox. So here I am."

"Didn't he tell you what he wanted?"

"Nothing, except that he wanted to make some change in his will. He talked to me himself, and he seemed somewhat excited."

"You know he's been threatening to disinherit Thorn," I said tentatively. "Because she wants to marry Franklin Knox."

He stroked his white mustache meditatively.

"Why, do you suppose?" I asked, when he didn't say anything. "You'd think just off-hand it's the kind of a match that would please him most. Instead he's been carrying on just as he did about Dan and Joan Frazier."

Mr. Rand shook his head.

"That's one of the great mysteries of human conduct, my dear. The way parents and guardians act towards young people when they decide to marry. I'm convinced in my heart, though I don't like to admit it, that my two daughters have literally thrown themselves away. You'll do the same thing, some day."

"It's more than that with Mr. Sutton," I replied stubbornly. "I think it's the same sort of thing as Aunt Charlotte's cabin, and everything else he's got. He's bent on being master of everything, human or otherwise, in the place. Just as he would probably have given the college something if he could be sure of being the only one who did. Did he leave us anything, by the way—or is that a professional secret?"

Mr. Rand smiled ironically.

"We need a bass drum," I said, "and Miss Henry tells me somebody has stolen the Decameron from the library."

Again Mr. Rand smiled.

"We can just about make the two of them, I should think," he said. "Sutton was rather a practical joker. I'm afraid it'll be a blow to Knox. Fortunately, however, the Guggenheim people are definitely interested now—we can forget about Mr. Sutton. Except to find out who shot him."

I was, I'm afraid, a little more interested in what the Guggenheim Foundation was going to do for us than in Mr. Sutton's death. But Mr. Rand wouldn't be drawn, and furthermore he swore me to absolute secrecy until Commencement.

"What I want of you, young lady," he said gravely, "is to tell me how much you know, from Thorn and the others, of what's been going on around here lately. Sutton's not been himself for quite a while."

"Oh," I said. "That's undoubtedly . . ."

A tap on the door cut me short.

"Come in!" Mr. Rand boomed.

It was Mr. Sullivan.

"I wonder if you'd come with me, Mr. Rand, and Mrs. Niles too," he said. "I've got something here I want you to see."

We followed him across the hall and into the library. He was being extremely deliberate. I almost had to stop still in front of the chair where Mr. Sutton had sat. I couldn't help seeing the stain on the wing of the chair. As a matter of fact it did have some horrible fascination for me, and I must have looked at it longer than I should have done; I felt Mr. Sullivan looking intently at me. Our eyes met for a second. His were perfectly impersonal. I thought that he would undoubtedly hang his grandmother if necessary.

"This way, sir," he said, motioning Mr. Rand to the far end of the room.

We followed him towards the front windows, and stopped when he stopped, in front of Mr. Sutton's desk.

There were several neat piles of papers on top of it, but Mr. Sullivan seemed not interested in them. Instead he raised the leather-eared blotting pad and pointed to a slip of paper from a memorandum pad that was on top of some other papers between it and the desk-top.

"Read it," he said, "but don't touch it."

Both of us bent over. I recognized Mr. Sutton's precise beautiful hand. He had written:

Memo. for Rand April 25

1. Remove ranch from residue.
2. Stipulate removal of incumbent, otherwise $200,000 trust, chair of anthropology, void.
3. Cut T. in event marriage before 36.
4. Remove F. from any benefit in toto.

My heart skipped a beat. I read that second item again, and felt the blood pounding against my temples. My first impulse was one of blind red anger. What had Ben done to him? I had no notion; but it seemed to me horribly unfair, in some way, for any man to have such a club with which to beat another.

Suddenly I realized that both Mr. Rand and Mr. Sullivan were watching me. They both looked away at precisely the same moment, Mr. Rand to study the memorandum again, Mr. Sullivan to examine the heavily carved cornice of the room.

"What time was it that you left here last night, Mrs. Niles?" asked Mr. Sullivan. He turned from the cornice to the matter in hand with obvious nonchalance, but still I didn't realize in the least what he was so plainly getting at.

"I left here a little before one o'clock, with Mr. Niles."

"And you returned?"

"At three, with Thorn Carter."

"What did you do in between those times?"

"I went to bed, went to sleep, and woke up at 2.15 by my bedside clock. It may be a few minutes off one way or another. I went downstairs and let Thorn in. We talked until some time after 2.30."

"Mrs. Niles," he went on, with a friendliness that I now began to take a little alarm at, "several people have testified —at least they've told me—that you had on tennis slippers when you came over here."

"That's quite correct."

"And stockings."

"Yes."

"Now, Mrs. Niles. Did you go upstairs and put on stockings and tennis shoes after Miss Thorn Carter came to your house? Or did you already have them on?"

I looked at him in surprise. I'm afraid I hesitated a little too long. His eyes flickered triumphantly.

"They were in the closet downstairs," I said. "I slipped them on when I got my coat."

"Do you keep stockings in the downstairs closet, Mrs. Niles—just for emergencies?"

"They happened to be socks, not stockings really," I said. "They were there by accident. I'd worn them over a pair of silk stockings when I was playing tennis with the children the day before. They were stuffed in my shoes; I just slipped them on."

"Why did you put on tennis slippers at all, Mrs. Niles?"

"Because I didn't care to clump over here in green satin mules, Mr. Sullivan," I said acidly.

"What are mules? Bedroom slippers?"

"Yes."

"Did you leave your mules in the closet?"

"Yes."

"Did you take them upstairs with you when you got back at four o'clock?"

"No. I didn't think of them."

Mr. Rand stirred and cleared his throat, gently but ominously. Mr. Sullivan however was bent on his course.

"In that case, Mrs. Niles, can you explain why one of my men who went to your house this morning was unable to find your green bedroom slippers in the downstairs closet?"

"Probably because the maid had put the slippers in their proper place." I was extremely annoyed at what seemed an unwarrantable intrusion into my house.

"In which case we would assume that she would have put the tennis slippers and your coat downstairs, in their proper place, in the closet."

"Except that she does the downstairs first," I replied.

"In that case, Mrs. Niles, perhaps you can explain this."

He held out a folded piece of paper.

"We found this in the pocket of your tweed coat."

I took it and opened it. Like the memorandum I had just read, it was in Mr. Sutton's unmistakable handwriting. I read it. There was no salutation.

I want you to see me before morning. I shall wait for you in the library. Important.

D. S.

XIX

Obvious as it was, I still didn't realize what he was driving at.

Mr. Rand said, "Sullivan, I suggest that you give Mrs. Niles a chance to explain that paper before you jump to a conclusion."

"Mrs. Niles will have plenty of opportunity to explain several things," Mr. Sullivan said, slightly nettled by Mr. Rand's calm assumption of leadership.

Then I did see what it was all about. I looked from one to the other of them in blank amazement.

"Do you mean, Mr. Sullivan," I demanded incredulously, "that you think *I* shot Mr. Sutton?"

Mr. Sullivan's professional suavity quickly returned.

"I merely suggest, Mrs. Niles," he said calmly, "that you had the two prime requisites for the State's Attorney's case —which he is bound to look for. Motive"—he tapped the memorandum sharply—"and . . . Opportunity."

"Oh," I said weakly, and sat down in Mr. Sutton's desk chair.

Then I did a preposterous thing that absolutely convinced Mr. Sullivan he was right. He thinks to this day that I shot Daniel Sutton to keep the Sutton Chair of Anthropology at Landover College, with its stipend of $8,000, open for my husband. I began to laugh. It seemed to me perfectly, hilariously, funny that anybody would think that I'd shoot Daniel Sutton. Perhaps, however, if I'd known about that second provision of the memorandum, I would have done.

"When did you get this note from Mr. Sutton, Mrs. Niles?" asked Mr. Sullivan, frowning heavily at what seemed to him my indecent conduct.

"I didn't get it," I said promptly. "I found it."

Then it occurred to me on what a dangerous course I'd

embarked, and I decided I'd better say nothing more until I'd thought it over. I remember feeling a momentary glow of self-righteousness. Ben says I\ never think until I'm through speaking, and that I play the best game of bridge of anyone he knows who never thinks about a card until it's down. At any rate I did think at this moment that laying my cards on the table, as Mr. Sullivan would say, would involve Thorn, and the business of the locked gate, and Heaven knows what else. When I picked the note up it had seemed obvious that Reverdy had dropped it when he stood under the light counting his bills. Now it seemed fairly clear that it was Thorn. It would account certainly for her staying behind when the others went upstairs, as Colonel Arbuthnot-Howe said she did.

So I stopped where I was.

"If I'm suspected, Mr. Sullivan," I said calmly, "I think I'd better not say anything more until . . ."

I didn't want to say "Until I've seen Thorn." So I said, as I do to servants when I haven't decided just what to say, "Until I've consulted Mr. Niles."

It worked just as well in this case, except that with servants I go upstairs, think it over and come down and tell them that Mr. Niles has decided the matter thus and so. I couldn't make a bee-line to Thorn, and then come back, obviously; so I fished in my sweater pocket and found a limp package of Chesterfields. Mr. Rand lighted one for me.

"I think you're wise, Mrs. Niles," he said gravely. "Please consider me entirely at your service."

"Thanks, Mr. Rand," I said. Then I turned to Mr. Sullivan. "May I go now, or are you taking me to jail?"

At this point the young man came in with several telegrams, which he handed to Mr. Sullivan, who tore them open, got out his horn-rimmed spectacles and read them with exasperating deliberation. I don't know what made me suppose he would read them aloud. At last he folded them all up neatly, took off his glasses and returned them to his pocket, and turned to us.

"No finger-prints on either telephone—wiped clean. None on the safe. Gun, a .38, fired about three feet off. That doesn't get us much forrarder."

He stuffed the telegrams in his coat pocket.

"Mrs. Niles, you'll be at home if I want to see you, I suppose?" he said cautiously.

"I won't be far away, at any rate, Mr. Sullivan."

I pressed out my cigarette in the white jade ashtray on the desk. Mr. Sullivan looked at the gradually writhing butt—it was almost half a cigarette—then he looked at me. I looked at the white half-smoked column, with the tiny crimson tip from my lips, and then looked at him.

"Don't tell me you found a cigarette with lipstick on it at the feet of the victim," I said mockingly.

Mr. Rand smiled. Mr. Sullivan did not. His pale eyes flickered.

"I didn't, Mrs. Niles," he said. "But Colonel Arbuthnot-Howe did. Like to see it?"

He produced an envelope from somewhere. I began to think, from the way he had of suddenly producing things, that he wore saddle-bags. He opened the gummed flap and let the contents roll out on a piece of foolscap on the table. It was a cigarette, much like mine, half-smoked, with a faint crimson stain at the end. Mr. Rand and I leaned over and examined it closely. Mr. Sullivan watched with a gleam of mild satisfaction in his eyes.

"It won't do, Mr. Sullivan," I said. "It's at least three shades darker. That, I should say, is what is known as Red Ruby. I use Red Geranium, or something quite lighter. It's a fine point, Mr. Sullivan."

"I'm aware of that, Mrs. Niles. But it does belong to one of you ladies."

"That's a fair assumption," I conceded sweetly.

"So that if it doesn't belong to you, it must belong to Miss Thorn. Anyway, from what my daughter tells me the darker you are the darker the shade of lipstick."

"Something of the sort, anyway."

"Then you agree that it belongs to Thorn Carter."

"I don't see why I shouldn't. She admits freely that she talked to her uncle before she went to bed, and before she got up again and came over to my house."

He looked at me with a slow twisted smile.

"She does, does she?" he said.

My heart sank. Had I said too much? I was very glad when Mr. Rand took my arm and said he'd walk home with me if I was going now.

As a matter of fact I wanted most to see Thorn, and find out just what her position was, and how much and what she had told or intended to tell Mr. Sullivan. It never occurred to me even for a moment that she'd begin at the beginning and stop at the end. More than that, I wasn't particularly anxious to go home. I hadn't the slightest desire to have Ben screw up his face with his air of amused tolerance at the indiscretions of a total incompetent. "Dear little Martha, aren't *you* a one." That he'd ever take me more seriously, even when

I was accused of murder, was the last thing I ever thought of. Nevertheless, Mr. Rand was going home with me, so home I went.

We went out the front door without seeing anybody, except the young man and the state policeman on the porch. Rich was still at the gate. The crowd had dispersed with the arrival of a second policeman, who at this moment was talking to a couple of college students on the campus across the street. We set out towards my house.

"Look here, Mr. Rand," I said abruptly. "I've got to see Thorn, and I don't want to see my husband."

"In that case I'd advise you to talk to me."

There was a twinkle in his eye.

"All right," I said. "I will."

And I did. I told him about seeing Reverdy counting something that looked like a roll of bills, under the lamp on King Charles Street. We had reached the intersection of King Charles Street and York Road, and I pointed to the lamp post.

"It was right there," I said. "He came out of the gate—at least I assumed he did. I heard a click, then I saw him emerge."

I told him about my going to bed and being waked up by Thorn about 2.15.

"She was in a ghastly state. She'd had a quarrel with her uncle before she went to bed. Then she thought she heard something downstairs, and went to see what it was. As far as I can make out, she got the wind up about something else she thought she heard, or did hear, and dashed out the garden door down the path to the gate."

"This gate?" Mr. Rand asked, indicating the one down the road.

I nodded.

"Let's take a look, then."

We turned down until we came even with the great iron grill where Thorn and I had stood not twelve hours ago.

"It's locked," he said, trying the handle.

"That's the funny thing about it that I didn't want to tell Mr. Sullivan. It's always locked. When we decided to go back to the house, we came this way, and it *was* locked. Thorn swore she'd just come out."

"Then plainly somebody else must have been there and locked it," Mr. Rand said meditatively. He peered through the bars along the wooded vista that finally ends in leafy greenness.

"Then we started back towards York Road, and it was then

that I found the note from Mr. Sutton. I stuck it in my pocket without letting Thorn see it. I thought Reverdy'd dropped it."

"You didn't know what was in it until Sullivan showed it to you just now?"

"No. I forgot all about it after I saw Mr. Sullivan."

He chuckled. "I decided," he said, "that if you were that good an actress I shouldn't believe another word you said."

I ignored his imputation on my veracity.

"And that's another funny thing," I said. "Thorn pulled the bell at the other gate, and *some one* let us in."

Mr. Rand nodded.

"Thorn, I take it," he remarked after a little, "has something to hide. What about yourself?"

"Not a thing. My life's an open book," I replied solemnly, raising my right hand.

"I fancy Thorn's is too, in spite of all this to-do."

"I'm sure it is. Franklin's in town—that's reason enough for the way she's been acting."

He nodded sagely.

"Yes. I'm inclined to think that Sullivan's over-estimating the rigors of the course of true love. Not that I wish to underestimate them, by any means," he added quickly.

"They're pretty hard. Susan and I are getting jolly well fed up with this Thorn-Franklin business," I returned. But he was thinking about something else.

"Who is this Baca person, now, that Susan was telling me about on the way down," he asked when we had got in the house. I discovered to my relief that Ben and Dr. Parr his dog—an ill-favored but amiable beast—had gone to the library until lunch. We settled ourselves in their study. I say "their" because they bury the bones of their calling in it and defy anyone to disturb them.

I rang the bell for Lillie to bring Mr. Rand some White Rock.

"I can explain Mr. Baca," I said. "He told me this morning that he had practically completed his arrangements with Mr. Sutton about this Mexican ranch he came to see him about. He said it was unfortunate that Mr. Sutton had died, and he almost died himself when I told him Mr. Sutton had been murdered. I'll swear he didn't know it before."

Mr. Rand thought about that. Then he got up rather abruptly, after draining his tall glass.

"I wonder if I'm not beginning to see what this is all about, Mrs. Niles?" he said, reaching for his grey bowler hat. "You've just reminded me incidentally of something I must

94

do right away. Like Mr. Sullivan I assume I can find you here when I want you?"

"Here or near by," I said. "Where shall I find you when I'm arrested?"

"You won't be—yet," he said.

XX

I took off my hat and sat down at the telephone to arrange for some other member of the Landover Book Club to take the Friday meeting. It seemed to me that it might be less embarrassing than if I waited and had to have Ben call everybody up Thursday night and say, "I'm so sorry, but Mrs. Niels won't be able to have the Club to-morrow. She's in the county jail."

I thought of several persons who wouldn't try to keep me to find out the latest news, and was still thinking when the phone rang. It was Susan. Thorn was awake and wanted to see me. Would I come? Mr. Sullivan had gone home for lunch.

I said I'd be delighted in that case, and put my hat on again. I was just getting out the front door when Lillie intercepted me. She wanted to know if we were still having a dinner party that night and who would we ask in place of the Suttons? That necessitated considerable rearrangement; and by the time I was ready to leave there was another ring at the door. I went to see who it was; and it was Franklin Knox, looking as if he'd been put through a wringer.

"Hullo," I said. "Where've you been?"

"I've been around, if you really want to know, to see that damned lawyer."

"Mr. Hawkins?"

"No less," he muttered, and threw his hat in one chair and sat down in another, his head on his hands, elbows on his knees.

"Come in Ben's study, Franklin," I said, "and tell me about it. I'm in a hurry, I'm just on my way to see Thorn."

He groaned, got up and with a gesture of despair followed me into the study, where he flopped down again, on the sofa.

I was amazed at the heavy lines in his extraordinarily fine strong face. His eyes were bloodshot, he hadn't shaved. He lit a cigarette and brushed back the lock of hair that like his father's always managed to get out of place and down on his high forehead. What with his brown suit that hadn't been to the presser for several days, he looked absolutely used up.

"Look, Martha," he said desperately. "Do you think Thorn had anything to do with this?"

"Lord, no!" I exclaimed incredulously, as if he were the first person who'd ever suggested such a thing.

"Does Sullivan?"

"Mr. Sullivan thinks I did it."

"You? What for?"

"Unwritten law. Right of every woman to protect her nest. My husband, it seems, under a will or something, stands to get the stipend from a two hundred thousand dollar chair of Anthropology when the old man died. It seems that last night or before Sutton decided he shouldn't have it, and was about to change his will. I, with my well-known clairvoyance, knew this, and Bang! Mr. Sutton is dead. Ben gets enough to pay the rent with and send the children to school. I go dry-eyed to the gallows. What could be clearer?"

"Don't be an idiot, Martha," he groaned. "This is serious. Look here. I'm a lawyer, and I know just how much good a phoney confession is, but if Thorn's in danger I'll say I did it. And by God I'll prove I did it too."

"Swell. Then I won't have to go dry-eyed to the gallows. We do hang us in Maryland, don't we."

"Listen, Martha. I tell you it's serious."

He looked around, then leaned closer to me.

"Thorn and I had a quarrel. It was my fault."

"I've heard all about it. It was Thorn's fault."

"No. It was mine."

"All right. As a matter of fact if either one of you had a lick of sense . . ."

"Oh I know. But anyway, it's over now. Listen. I came down last night and tried to get in touch with her. I didn't want Sutton to give her a going over, so Dad said he'd go over after dinner and take her a message. She phoned me about 12.10, I guess, and said she'd meet me down at the King Charles Street gate when everybody went to bed. She said she'd have Rich or somebody unlock the gate and I could come in and wait at . . . at our place."

"I see," I said.

"I couldn't read or do anything. So I went down there about 12.30 and waited. Pretty soon I heard somebody. But I know Thorn's step, it wasn't her. I was in the shadow of a tree, so I laid low. Somebody whistled. Then I saw Hawkins come to the gate."

"Reverdy? From the street?"

"Yes. He tried the gate and came in. I heard him talking to somebody, but I couldn't see who it was. Pretty soon I heard him say 'Mr. Wally,'; then I heard 'Charlotte.' That was that. Then Wally began to get pretty sore. He said 'You lay off, you damned scarecrow, or I'll murder you.' There was an argument. Finally Hawkins left. I guess that was about 1.00."

I nodded.

"It was; I saw him leave. We were just getting home.".

"Well, Wally heard me, I think. I heard him hoofing it back pronto to the house. Well, I stuck around then, until I couldn't stand it any longer. I thought she couldn't get away or maybe she'd met Wally, or something. I went along as quietly as I could to the house."

I looked at him.

"What time was that, Franklin?"

"That's the point. I looked at my watch at a little after 1.30; and just as I did I thought I heard a shot. I was still way down in the back garden, on the path. I stayed there. About five minutes later I saw a man come out on the porch and look around. The hall light was on. What with that and the moon I could see him pretty well. I don't know who it was—a big fellow though. In a minute Wally came out there too."

So it was like that, I thought.

"Well, I got the idea of clearing out then. But while I was there the big fellow slipped over to the side of the porch by the back drawing room window, and Wally cut down and around the house to the left, around the kitchen wing."

I was naturally listening to this open-mouthed. Was it possible that Colonel Arbuthnot-Howe . . . ?

"Then I thought I couldn't get out, I didn't know what could have happened to Thorn. I went up behind the kitchen, up on the porch and inside. It was then the funny thing happened. Just as I got in the light went off, and I was pretty sure I heard the library door close. I tipped over and tried to open it, but it was locked from inside. I thought I'd turn on the lights and see what the devil was up, when I heard somebody coming down the stairs. I thought it would look funny for me to be there just then, so I stepped in the recess of the front drawing room door and held my breath."

So Thorn was right, I thought.

"I thought it was Thorn, but I didn't want to frighten her. I didn't say anything. I forgot the switch was right there by my hand, or I'd have turned on the light. Before I knew it she'd gone around the staircase and was out the garden door.

Then I came to my senses. And just at that time I heard somebody in the back drawing room. No mistake about that. I kept still. Then another queer thing happened: there was a definite smell of cordite in the hall. I hadn't noticed it before. It got faint again. I knew I was getting in deeper than I'd planned, but I didn't know how to get out."

"What time was that?"

He frowned in intent recollection.

"The clock struck two when Thorn came down. I remember the bell sort of drowned out her steps or I'd have been surer it was her. I guess this happened five to ten minutes later. Well anyway, I got out and started down to the path after Thorn. I looked back in a minute, and the hall light was on again. Whoever it was was just waiting for me to get out."

I took a deep breath, and glanced at my wrist watch. He didn't stop.

"I cut down along the path after Thorn. Once I thought I heard her running, then I thought I heard the gate click; but when I got there she'd disappeared. I didn't like to stick around too long. I whistled but she didn't answer."

"She was here," I said.

He nodded.

"I saw a light and guessed she was here. Well, I stuck around a few minutes under your kitchen window. It seemed useless to stay, when I knew where she was, so I decided I'd go home and phone to her at your house. I was just leaving when I saw Wally come out of the gate, look around, go over by the lamppost, take a piece of paper out of his pocket, run his handkerchief over it and drop it under the post."

I stared at him in consternation. It dawned on me that I wasn't very clever. Wally had deliberately set a trap, and I had walked into it, bag and baggage.

"Go on," I said.

"He went back and through the gate. I heard him lock it. Just then you and Thorn came down the street and tried the gate. You then went towards York Road, and you picked up Wally's paper and put it in your pocket. By that time I'd decided to let you go on and not explain to Thorn until today."

I looked at him a long time. Then I said, "In that case I'd explain to her now, and then both of you explain to Mr. Sullivan. It'll make things a lot simpler."

He shook his head miserably.

"What's wrong now?" I demanded.

"Do you think she'll see me?"

"Good Lord!" I groaned. "For Heaven's sake go on over

98

and see her. I'll call up and tell her you're coming. Good bye!"

He hadn't been gone five minutes when there was another ring at the door. It was Bill Sutton this time.

"Look here, Martha," he began hastily. "I came by the Charles Street gate and they don't know I've gone."

"Yes?" I said, and waited.

"I unlocked the gate for Thorn last night. She was going to see Franklin as soon as she could get out."

"Yes," I said. "Franklin was just here. You'd have met him if you'd come down York Road."

"Well, look here," he went on quickly, "I left the key in the gate, and Thorn was to lock it. She told me it was locked when she came back from here, and this morning the key's in its place on the hook in the kitchen hyphen."

"Wally put it there," I said. I told him what Franklin had just told me about Wally's locking the gate.

"The dirty skunk," he said savagely. "Some day he'll get what's coming to him. But Martha—do you think Franklin shot my father? Because if he did I don't blame him."

He stared rigidly into the empty grate.

"I'm sure he didn't. However, he's just got through telling me he's going to say he did, and prove it, if there's danger of Thorn's being involved."

That appealed to Bill's movie soul.

"Good fellow!" he muttered.

"Stupid idiot, you mean. If he'd not been the perfect fool, Thorn wouldn't be in this mess, to begin with."

Bill was thinking about something else. I have a hard time remembering that he's twenty-four and through Princeton, and quite a capable young fellow even if he has unruly brown hair like Thorn's and brown eyes like hers. They were puzzled when he turned to me.

"What do you think of that Mexican, Martha?" he asked earnestly.

"I think he's a *very* nice man," I said, with more conviction than I should have thought I felt. "Why?"

"Well, that ass of a Susan has done nothing all morning but take him ice packs and calves-foot jelly and change the radio for him. She even went down in the cellar and got some of Dad's pre-war claret for him."

"Why not?"

"Why not?"

He repeated my words with infinite disgust.

"She's only known the fellow two days."

99

"That's a long time when you're twenty, Bill," I replied philosophically. "Mr. Baca is very handsome and perfectly charming and polite and all that sort of thing. I imagine Susan found it a change from being called an idiot and an ass and a half-wit. I know I would."

He looked at me with the strangest, most pathetic look in his eyes.

"But Martha," he said plaintively. It sounded very odd in an All-American quarter. "She knows we don't mean it. She's just a kid."

"Yes. I know all about that. I've got six older brothers myself."

XXI

Ben came in for lunch shortly after Bill left. I gathered he hadn't been doing anything very taxing at the library. He had a midiron in his hand and Dr. Parr had an old golf ball in his mouth. Ben put his club in the bag in the closet and came in to the living room.

"I was just talking to Mr. Rand," he said casually.

I prepared for the worst.

"What did he say?"

"He says they've got a gift of fifty thousand for the library, from a woman in New York, a friend of his wife's. It'll take a load off the library committee's mind."

"Oh," I said weakly.

"We need a lot of books for new courses."

"I suppose so. What else did Mr. Rand say?"

"Nothing. He was just coming out of Aunt Charlotte's. Oh yes. He said Sullivan had discovered you had a motive for shooting Sutton. I told him to tell Sullivan he was demented, you actually were fond of the old boy."

"What did he say to that?"

"Nothing. Seemed to think it was queer. When's lunch?"

There's never any use of my being annoyed with Ben, or trying to find out anything that's happened. So I gave up after I'd made one more attempt.

"Did you see Dr. Knox this morning?"

"Yes. He's afraid Saunders isn't going to pull through in Math. 21. If he doesn't he won't be able to play football next fall. I guess the old guard's after him again."

"Wouldn't it be a lot simpler if they get after Saunders

and make him pass Math. 21 now? It'd save a month of meetings and moilings next fall. Can't somebody give a lecture on preventative medicine or something?"

He shrugged his shoulders. "Oh well, it doesn't matter. Knox has to have something of this sort to worry about. He thinks the endowment business is pretty well settled."

"That's good. If we get the endowment settled, and the business of who can play on what teams settled, and money for the library, I should say life in the Niles family would be fairly smooth. But I suppose something else would come up."

"That's life," Ben replied with simple irony. "I suppose there's baked apples for dessert."

I ignored that, and we went back to the subject of the library budget, and ended lunch with an account of Dugan's sprained shoulder that unfortunately would keep him out of the lacrosse game with the Hopkins in the Baltimore Stadium on Saturday. I wish I were as single minded as Ben. I left the table feeling that he wouldn't care in the least if I were put in jail. After brooding over that a few minutes, I pulled myself together with the knowledge that he would care, because he wouldn't be able to find anything if I weren't around. I suppose that's a fairly solid foundation for domestic tranquillity. Anyway, I had other things more important to do at the moment.

I was still doing them at four o'clock when Susan Atwood appeared. She was troubled about something, I gathered from the clouded blue eyes that are normally as clear as cornflowers.

I was in my room at my desk making out checks for the butcher, baker and candlestick maker, and tearing up some old letters that I didn't care to have discussed by the whole town in the event that Mr. Sullivan decided to do any more searching among my effects. I put down my pen and turned around in my chair. Susan flopped down on the chaise longue and adjusted the pillows under her head.

"How's your patient?" I inquired by way of conversation.

"All right, I guess. Mr. Rand is talking to him now. Or he was when I left."

She answered my question listlessly and lapsed into a gloomy silence. I picked up my pen and went on making out a check for $15.32 to the butter and egg and chicken woman.

"Martha," she said tentatively.

"Yes."

"Martha, do you think Sebastien—I mean Mr. Baca—had anything to do with Uncle Dan's . . . death?"

101

I put down my pen, tore out the check, put it in an envelope, and turned around again.

Susan was sitting up, her chin in her hands, elbows on her knees, almost exactly as Franklin Knox had sat a few hours before. She was staring disconsolately out of the window.

"What makes you ask that, Sue?"

"Everybody's being so funny about him. I'm about the only person that's been near him today, except you. And I *did* see him last night, of course. And that's one of the things that bothers me. You see, I said I'd seen him, and Dan and you and Colonel Arbuthnot-Howe all heard me, but Mr. Sullivan hasn't spoken to him or to me either."

"Maybe he's on another trail."

"Yes, I know. I just heard him telling a reporter from the *Sun* that he was leaving no stone unturned," she said dryly, and lapsed into another preoccupied silence.

"In that case he'll get around to both of you sooner or later," I assured her.

"Sooner, I guess. Mr. Rand asked me after lunch when I'd seen him. I told him about two o'clock. He wanted to know what I was doing up at that time."

"Well, what were you?" I asked after a bit.

"I was thinking."

It was said very soberly. I remembered what I'd just said to Bill about being polite to Susan, repressed the obvious reply and waited for her to elaborate.

"I was sitting by the window looking down the terrace at the water," she went on dreamily. "It was beautiful. You know, Martha. The fringe of trees along each side of the lawn was deep black, and the water was sort of shimmery. It wasn't as bright as it was earlier, but it was sort of luminous. You know?"

I looked at Susan with certain misgivings. It was, I gathered, the first time she'd ever seen the beauties of nature. I didn't know how long this rhapsody would take. She was still gazing sadly into space.

"I don't think Sebas—Mr. Baca had anything to do with it, Martha."

"Call him Sebastien, Susan," I said. "It's easier."

"It's a nice name, isn't it?" she said with a sudden smile.

"Mm," I said. My misgivings increased a hundred-fold. "Where was he, by the way, when you saw him?"

"He was down by the path to the King Charles Street gate, just in the shrubs. He sort of cut around and up by the kitchen. I guess he went across the porch and through the drawing room to the wing—or he could have gone across

102

and in the outside door. But then he wouldn't have known the way, I shouldn't think, would you?"

I shook my head. There was something wrong here, that was obvious. Nevertheless I didn't want to tell Susan too much.

"Are you sure it *was* Mr. Baca, Sue?" I asked.

She raised her troubled young eyes to mine. They were charmingly blank.

"I *thought* so."

"Are you sure?"

"No, I'm not, of course. It was a funny light, but it was a man and he was tall, slim, dark, and . . . there's nobody else like that."

I didn't say anything. Gradually the expression in her eyes changed from bewilderment through a whole series of emotions to triumphant comprehension.

"Martha, it wasn't Sebastien at all!"

Her voice quickened.

"That was Franklin! That's what's the matter with Thorn. She thinks Franklin shot Uncle Dan! My *dear!!*"

"And Franklin thinks Thorn did it," I added.

"What rot," said Susan with finality. She lapsed slowly back into her former state.

My afternoon was then punctuated by another silence. Her next question took me back to my rapidly growing suspicions.

"Martha," she said without looking up, "have you ever been in love?"

"Many times," I replied without hesitation.

"No, I mean *really*."

"So did I."

She puckered her smooth forehead and said, with tears not very far off, "I wish you'd be serious, Martha. Nobody'll *ever* talk to me seriously."

"I'm perfectly serious, Susan," I said. "You start falling in love about your age, or younger, and you keep it up until you marry somebody. Some people continue after that, but that's to be avoided unless you fall in love again with the person you've married. That sometimes happens."

She thought over the first part of what I'd said. The last part clearly did not interest her. No doubt some day it would seem infinitely more important; but that was ten years off.

"Martha," she said wistfully, after a minute or so, "isn't it funny that suddenly you see things you never saw before, even though things have been right in front of your nose all your life?"

I nodded. "Yes, it's funny."

"It's like the garden last night. I never noticed before how many sounds there are at night, and how gorgeous it smells with the lilacs and roses and what a pleasant little sound the box trees make. Last night the air was like velvet. Do you know what I mean?"

Her eyes shone like two blue stars in the creamy pallor of her face under the crown of smooth gold ahir. What a contrast they'd make, I thought. Sebastien Baca was so dark.

"What did you think of, Sue?"

"I thought of the last time I saw my mother, when I was very little," she said, her lips quivering in wistful curves. "It was one night. She had on a dark blue velvet dress. She came to kiss me good night, and I reached out and touched her dress. I liked the feel of it, and it had a very lovely perfume. Well, last night was like that. I just closed my eyes and I could feel the velvet all around me."

I didn't say anything, but I suppose really that's the way mothers would like to be remembered.

In a minute she was practical downright Susan again.

"Martha, can you be in love with anybody without them being in love with you?"

Susan's syntax was something that nobody had ever bothered with very much.

"That's a question, Sue," I replied helpfully. "I was terribly in love with my Greek professor, and I don't think he knew I was on earth."

"But I mean *really*."

Perhaps she was right. That seemed very real when I was seventeen.

"Ordinarily, I'd say not, in that case," I told her "But you can't generalize, my dear. It's best to wait and see."

She nodded, her eyes clouding again, the tiny frown puckering her brows. Her lips drooped at the corners.

"I suppose so. But it seems very stupid."

"Better stupid than shocking," I said sententiously.

Suddenly she smiled impishly.

"Or else very clever," she said. "I'm going home. Will you come with me? Oh, by the way—Mr. Rand sent me to get you. Mr. Sullivan wanted him to bring you to Sullivan's office at the court house at 4:15."

I looked at my watch. It was then quarter to five.

XXII

I sent Susan back to Seaton Hall and telephoned Mr. Rand.

"Mistah Nathan he'd in conf'rence with Miss Mildred an' Mistah Dan," Lafayette's high wheezy voice piped across the wire. "Ah'll ask him call you direc'ly he come downstairs, Miss."

"Very well, Lafayette," I replied. I was about to put down the phone when I realized that the old man was still at his end and that he probably had something to say.

"How is everything?" I added. He would never say it, if he did have something to tell, without an opening.

"It's all right, Miss," he said significantly. "Only Mistah Sullivan he's been raisin' time here 'cause he cain't see Miss Thorn."

"Let him raise it then, Lafayette."

" 'Deed an' Ah will, Miss. 'Deed Ah ain' goin' stop him."

I put the phone down, wondering just what kind of time Mr. Sullivan had been raising, and thinking it was a useless waste of his own. He could hardly expect to be very impressive with anyone who knew as many legal circumventions as Mr. Rand about, or indeed with anyone who chose to be as stubborn as Thorn could be when she did choose. It was however perfectly clear that his business with me in his court house office was not as urgent as I'd assumed, or Mr. Rand wouldn't be raisin' time with Thorn.

I changed my dress, got my hat and gloves and came down stairs to wait for what should happen. I picked up the afternoon paper and tried to read about what the local reporter called the most dastardly crime committed in the annals of our peaceful hamlet. He enlarged on Mr. Sutton's noble and useful life, mentioned the grief-stricken family, and added that Mr. Sutton's death left a gap in the community that would be well nigh impossible to fill. He ended by saying that the police were leaving no stone unturned to bring the dastard to justice. I used to think when I first came to Land-over that the Landover *Inquirer* was consciously funny. After reading it for six years and meeting the local reporter I changed my mind. No conscious intention could preserve so high an average.

I suppose all this was beginning to get on my nerves. Anyway, I was startled when I looked up and saw Lillie's black face and shiny eye thrown in high relief above the lamp on the low table beside me.

"Law me, did Ah scair you?" she inquired solicitously. She pads around the house in felt slippers anyway, so that one hardly ever hears her unless she's annoyed. Then she sounds like Pharaoh's army.

"Is they foun' out who done it?" she asked, looking behind her as if she expected "them" to hear her.

"Not yet."

"Well Ah guess they will, 'cause Ah seen Mistah Rand goin' in the telegram place when Ah was down gettin' some sugar you forget to ordah this mo'nin'. Ah guess he sent a powe'ful lot of telegraphs. He's in th' a powe'ful long time."

"Was he?" I turned the paper inside out to the society columns.

"Yass'm."

She went over and straightened the curtain. I watched her out of the corner of my eye. She moved a pillow on the sofa and put another in its place.

"They tells me Aunt Charlotte ain' goin' sell her house," she said after a moment.

"Isn't she?"

"No'm. They tell me that Reverdy Hawkins got money from somebody 'bout it an' that he's lef' town this mo'nin'."

"Really?" I asked with more interest than I usually show. "They tell me" is Lillie's expression either for a confidential authentic source or for simply the consensus of colored opinion gathered at the Methodist Episcopal Church in Westport.

"That's stupid of him," I said. "Now Mr. Sullivan will think he shot Mr. Sutton."

Lillie made some internal noise and shook her straight bear-greased thatch.

" 'Deed an' he won'," she said. "Mistah Sullivan, he knows Rev'dy won' do that."

After a moment she added, screwing up her black forehead, "Ain' the' a Mexican at the Hall?"

I nodded. She shook her head ominously.

"That's what they say," she observed. "They tell me they's treach'rous. Stick a knife in you fo' a nickel."

"I don't think this one would," I said, just as the door bell rang. "If that's Mr. Rand I'm all ready."

"Yass'm."

She padded quietly out. I heard her say "Come right in, suh, Miss Niles all ready."

It was Mr. Rand. I went out to meet him.

"Sullivan would like to see you at his office," he said. I thought he looked rather tired. I'd never noticed the deep furrows in his face before.

We went out, Lillie watching furtively through the curtain. I could imagine her storing this up for the Rosebud Circle (Daughters of the Nile) that night.

We got in my car. Mr. Rand somehow managed to get his legs folded up so as to give me room to shift gears without too much trouble.

"What's happened?" I asked.

"That's just what we're going to see," he said gravely. So gravely that I decided I'd better hold my peace. Which I did, remarkably enough, until we drew up in Court House Circle. I parked the car and we made our way through the crowd of men lolling on the benches and steps in front of the two-story brick building that houses Landover County's majesty of the law. On the steps we met Judge Duval. He shook hands with Mr. Rand and nodded to me. Judge Duval never fails to announce to every panel that women are at the bottom of all crimes. I thought it was very fitting that I should meet him now. They tell me—just as they tell Lillie—that in the drawing room he's the embodiment of chivalry; the point being that the minute women leave the house they're up to mischief. It's a simple creed, and Judge Duval follows it with a simplicity that would be admirable if one weren't a woman.

We went up to Mr. Sullivan's office and into the ante-room. Reverdy Hawkins was standing by the water cooler, ashy grey, smoothing the ruffled surface of his top hat.

"Good day, Mistah Rand; Good day ma'am."

He bowed with a jerk and looked very much like an exceedingly unhappy ostrich.

Mr. Rand looked him over carefully.

"I thought you left town, Reverdy," he said dryly.

"No suh, no suh!" Reverdy protested hastily. "Ah jus' ran up to Baltimo' for somethin'. Ah was comin' right back."

"I see. I'd been under the impression Mr. Sullivan had you brought back."

"A very nach'ral impression, suh. Ah came with Mistah Basil. Ah met him, an' we comes back togethuh. He thought Ah was goin' away, but Ah wasn' suh. No indeed."

Against the cloudy glass in the door marked "Mr. Sullivan" a shadowy figure moved briskly back and forth. It was taller than Mr. Sullivan and slimmer. Mr. Sullivan is short and rather stout. I watched it with a vague feeling of familiarity.

107

Suddenly the door opened and Franklin Knox burst out, Mr. Sullivan following complacently, a startling contrast to the white-lipped younger man.

At the sight of Mr. Rand's portly white-haired figure Franklin came to an abrupt stop. I gathered it was the first time they'd met that day. And it was a very curious meeting; and more curious to me now, when I look back on it, than it seemed then. Neither of them spoke. Their eyes, level with each other, met, and for a good minute neither of them wavered. Franklin's back was turned to me, so that I couldn't see the expression in his; but I could see Mr. Rand's blue eyes looking steadily into the younger man's. They were appraising, counseling, questioning. It was almost as if Mr. Rand knew something he'd rather not know, and was putting it up to Franklin then and there before it was too late.

Mr. Sullivan interrupted.

"I'll see you in a few minutes, Hawkins," he said. "Wait outside."

He turned to Mr. Rand.

"Mr. Knox wishes to sign a confession," he said pleasantly, precisely as if he were ordering tea. "He says he shot and killed Mr. Sutton last night a few minutes after 1:30 o'clock."

Mr. Rand hadn't taken his eyes off Franklin's. Now I saw a flash of fire in them. Then a calculating questioning. Then a weary little smile.

He raised his brows.

"I see," he said. "Then the case is settled?"

"By no means," said Mr. Sullivan. "I'm convinced Mr. Knox is confessing to a crime he knows nothing about, in order to save Miss Thorn Carter."

Mr. Rand turned to Franklin. I thought for an instant that he was puzzled; but that seemed unlikely, under the circumstances. All of Franklin's conduct had been perfectly obvious.

Franklin's jaw, which had relaxed a little, clamped shut again until you could see the white ridges of its muscles.

"I shot Sutton, Mr. Sullivan," he said stubbornly. "That is all I have to say."

"Just wait a few minutes," Mr. Rand said quietly. "Let us talk this over with Mr. Sullivan."

He motioned to a chair, and Franklin, after a moment's hesitation, nodded and sat down. Mr. Sullivan held the door of his office open for us. I caught for an instant as I went past him the serious dark eyes in Franklin's sober American face. Not a flicker responded. I tried to imagine Ben sticking his head in a noose for me. I couldn't, some way. But Franklin

108

is just the stuff that heroes are made of. Not handsome in the sense that Mr. Baca is, but awfully fine, clean, intelligent and hardy looking.

Mr. Sullivan closed the door.

"Will you sit here, please, Mrs. Niles?" he said. He pointed to a chair facing the window where the late afternoon sun was shining.

I gathered that he was about to use psychology on me. I have a friend who uses that method in dealing with prospective clients.

"If you don't mind, Mr. Sullivan," I said sweetly, "I'll sit here. The light bothers my eyes."

He looked at me sharply, his grey eyebrows bristling like the hairs on a dog's back. I sat down with my back to the window. Mr. Rand smiled and sat in the chair meant for me. Mr. Sullivan settled himself in the squeaking fumed-oak swivel chair behind his desk.

XXIII

"Mr. Rand," began Mr. Sullivan in a fine man-to-man fashion, "you were Mr. Sutton's legal adviser, and I assume naturally"—he pronounced that and many other words exactly as Reverdy would—"that you want this thing cleared up and his murderer convicted."

Mr. Rand bowed his acquiescence with fine deliberateness. Mr. Sullivan went on.

"With that in mind, and because I've ceased to expect any intelligent cooperation from Mrs. Niles"—he bowed to me with ironic courtesy—"I have asked both of you here to tell you exactly where I stand in the matter as the representative of the State of Maryland."

He should have said "Free State of Maryland," of course, but we let that pass. We entered at once into the spirit of the thing, though I—and of course Mr. Rand—saw that this scene had been carefully rehearsed, the stage set beforehand.

"I want to tell you just what happened at Seaton Hall last night as I have it from every person there. Let me take them in order, now, beginning with Daniel Sutton."

If I'd been in the full light of the western glow, as Mr. Rand was, I must have looked rather startled at such a beginning. I hadn't thought of Mr. Sullivan as one likely to have communication with the departed. Mr. Rand however did not bat an eye.

"I have the incontestable evidence of Mr. Sutton's dead body. He was sitting, talking to someone he had no reason to fear. His posture, his face, his cigar, indicate this. His cigar especially; because everyone who knew Mr. Sutton even casually, as I did, knows that when he was . . . provoked, let us say, he chewed the end of his cigar violently. The tip of the cigar that Mr. Sutton was smoking that night shows no teeth marks; and it was half smoked.

"My next is Mrs. Niles. She went home at one o'clock and went to bed and to sleep. At 2:15 she arose and let Miss Thorn Carter in, talked with her about half an hour, went back to Seaton Hall with her; was with her when she rang the bell; and was admitted with her by Tim Healy—except that Tim Healy was dead. Entered the house, did not go in to speak to Mr. Sutton, whom she heard moving about—except that Mr. Sutton was dead. Helped Miss Thorn to bed, came down, heard someone in the back parlor, ran to the library, turned on the light, and found, quite by accident you understand, that Mr. Sutton was dead. Fainted, and was found by Colonel Arbuthnot-Howe, and later taken home by him."

This piece was spoken to gentlemen of the jury, and with an effective irony that even I could appreciate.

"Colonel Arbuthnot-Howe states that he was awakened by something, he thinks by someone passing his door. He heard a lady scream. He hurried downstairs, caught the lady as she fainted, then took her home."

Mr. Sullivan consulted a sheaf of papers on his desk.

"Dan Sutton heard a noise down stairs and came hurrying down from his room on the third floor, to see Colonel Arbuthnot-Howe leaning over Mrs. Niles, who was in a chair.

"Bill Sutton, asleep in the guest wing, heard a commotion and came through the open door from the hyphen to the back parlor, to see his brother standing by the wing chair with Colonel Arbuthnot-Howe, Mrs. Niles still seated.

"Susan Atwood asleep on the second floor heard a commotion, and came down to see all the above in the library."

Mr. Sullivan looked at me with hardly concealed pleasure, in thus offering my case to the mercies of my twelve imaginary peers.

"Miss Thorn Carter on the second floor slept soundly through all of this.

"Miss Mildred Carter—a very light sleeper—slept soundly through all of this. Also on the second floor.

"Mr. Baca, the Mexican, sleeping in a strange bed in a strange house, slept soundly through all of this.

"Mr. Wallace Fenton, on the third floor, the same."

Mr. Sullivan paused, with an affable air, to let this sink into our heads. Then suddenly he leaned forward, his eyes narrowing a little, his hands still folded quietly on the little pile of papers in front of him.

"We have here two possible conclusions," he said in a whisper. "Those people who slept quietly through all of this did not hear any noise, and it is therefore necessary to determine why Dan Sutton, Bill Sutton, Susan Atwood and Colonel Arbuthnot-Howe heard it so clearly. Or, the second group having heard the noise so plainly, it is necessary to explain why Miss Mildred Carter, Miss Thorn Carter, Mr. Fenton and Mr. Baca did *not* hear it."

Mr. Sullivan relaxed and sat back. So did I. It seemed to me to be, in a queer way, a fair statement of the case.

"Now," he went on, "we have a confession to this murder."

He picked up the paper on top of the pile and looked over it.

"Mr. Franklin Knox says that at 1:15 he climbed over the high wall at Seaton Hall, entered the study, had an argument with Mr. Sutton and shot him dead. He then went down to the river, threw the revolver out into the stream as far as he could, and came home, entering his father's house at 2:30 in the morning."

If Mr. Rand had not been sitting facing the light I shouldn't have caught the scarcely perceptible quickening of interest in his face and posture.

Mr. Sullivan, a furtive eye on me, paid no attention to him. After he made his first statement he looked down at the paper again meditatively and shrugged his shoulders.

"I have my men dragging the river," he went on. "We'll see shortly."

His face wore a grim anticipatory smile that would have done credit to Shylock whetting his knife.

"My last witness is Tim Healy."

As Mr. Sullivan's voice fell reverently I remembered his telling me the Saturday before to tell Mr. Sutton that if that mick watchman of his got tight again he'd land in the city cooler.

"Tim Healy doing his rounds at 1:30, came to a stop outside the open window of the library. Here is the evidence of that."

He handed me a thin paper disc. I looked blankly at it.

"Do you know what that is, Mrs. Niles?"

111

"No, I don't."

"It's a record from a watchman's punch clock. When Tim Healy started his rounds he pressed a button. The station and time are recorded automatically. What you see there is Station 1, Time 1:26."

I looked and saw the raised letters.

"Tim Healy started at 1:26 from the lodge. He walked up the path, saw a light that you and Thorn Carter did not see. He stepped to the open window and saw something that shocked him, shocked him so terribly that he died."

Mr. Sullivan tilted his chair back with a long drawn-out screaking.

"Healy's watch broke when he fell. But that is unsound as evidence. His watchman's clock he would have punched again in six or eight minutes—at 1:38 o'clock—at the King Charles Street gate, which is his Station 2, just as he has done every night for six years."

Leaf by leaf he turned over a three- or four-inch sheaf of the little discs from the watchman's clock.

"Station 1, 1:26," he read slowly. "Station 2, 1:38. Now ask yourself, Mrs. Niles, what Tim Healy saw that made his heart beat so rapidly that it exhausted itself and stopped beating forever."

He leaned forward and fixed me with his dissecting gaze.

"Simply ask yourself. And what is the answer?"

I began to wonder if he really wanted me to start a catechism aloud then and there. But he went on smoothly.

"We can dismiss anything so strange and unknown as to be horrible enough in itself so to affect him."

"As a matter of fact that isn't necessarily true," I said. Mr. Sullivan was so annoyed that I saw I'd got on the wrong line. But I went on.

"Tim believed entirely in fairies, goblins, witches and ghosts. It would have been perfectly possible for him to see anything."

Mr. Sullivan made a gesture of impatience.

"True, Mrs. Niles. But there was plainly some actual thing there. I meant it was actual enough to shoot Mr. Sutton. And since Sutton wasn't frightened in the least, I think we can assume that it was nothing either supernatural or horrible."

As that was plain enough I subsided into my proper rôle of auditor.

"And I put it to you that whoever it was that Tim Healy saw, it was someone he knew; someone he had faith and confidence in; someone he loved."

I nodded unhappily. Mr. Sullivan's eye brightened.

"Now let us run over the list of such people on your fingers, Mrs. Niles."

I had no intention of doing so, but he raised his own pudgy hand and ticked them off, beginning with his thumb.

Dan Sutton.

Bill Sutton.

Susan Atwood.

Miss Mildred Carter.

Mrs. Niles.

Thorn Carter.

Franklin Knox.

He stopped.

"What about Wallace Fenton?" I said.

He shook his head.

"That wouldn't have surprised Healy."

I looked up in amazement. He smiled. "I know more than you think I know, Mrs. Niles," I expected him to say; but he didn't.

"What about Mr. Sutton's two guests," Mr. Rand remarked.

Again Mr. Sullivan shook his head.

"No," he said. "That would not have been a shock to Tim." Which, of course, was perfectly true.

"Now," Mr. Sullivan went on, after a pause, "I'm going to take each of these seven that I've named, and tell you as much as I know about their motives in this matter.

"Dan Sutton. No motive that I've any proof of. Joan Frazier perhaps.

Bill Sutton—none.

Susan Atwood—none.

Miss Mildred Carter.

Here Mr. Sullivan paused. Then he said, "None."

"Mrs. Niles." He paused again and looked at me appraisingly. "Mrs. Niles has a very strong motive,—one of the strongest. If Mr. Sutton had died this evening instead of this morning at 1:30, your husband—hence you—would have lost $8,000 a year for life. A very powerful motive, Mrs. Niles."

I nodded.

"Very true," I said.

"Thorn Carter.—You said, Mr. Rand, that you had not a copy of Mr. Sutton's will with you?"

"I've sent for one," Mr. Rand said.

"Inasmuch as your client directed you to bring his will as he wished to change it, isn't it strange you didn't do so?"

I shuddered to hear him speak so directly to Mr. Rand.

He only smiled. "I've been dealing with Sutton for twenty-two years, Sullivan," he said. "I've changed his will in that period at least a hundred times. In late years, when I get a summons from Sutton, I come, make a memorandum of his wishes, go back to New York; and if, twenty-four hours later, I haven't ten telegrams telling me to disregard our recent conversations, I then make the change and forward the will for his signature."

Mr. Sullivan nodded his comprehension.

"Can you, then, tell me approximately how much Thorn Carter stood to lose if her uncle cut her out of the will?"

"The income for life on about three million dollars," Mr. Rand said simply.

"I think we have a motive for Thorn Carter, then," Mr. Sullivan returned. "I think we also have the same motive for Franklin Knox. I think this motive is insurmountable."

There was a long silence in the room.

"In that case," I asked, "what about Fenton?"

"I'm not overlooking that, Mrs. Niles. It's possible that it was Fenton that Tim Healy saw. He may have made a sudden move to stop him. His heart was bad, it may not have needed a great shock. It's possible that just the shock of seeing Sutton dead in the chair was enough to do it; Mr. Sutton may possibly have been killed half an hour before."

In that case, I thought, why carry on so? Presumably he had before ruled out Baca and Colonel Arbuthnot-Howe. But not at all. He seemed to sense my inward protest, for he said quietly, "No, Mrs. Niles, I have not disregarded anyone whatsoever."

I was about to demand what then, in the name of time, he was getting at, when there was a commotion in the outer office. The door opened, and young Basil, the state policeman, came in with another man. They were excited.

"Here you are, Mr. Sullivan!" Basil said. He stepped up to the table and laid down on it something wrapped in a piece of gunny sack.

Mr. Sullivan waited without a word until the door of his office, on its automatic slide, clicked shut. Then he took up the object and opened the burlap wrapping. It was a revolver, covered with mud.

We stared at it. I don't know which of us was the most astounded.

"Where'd you get this?" Mr. Sullivan barked.

"In the river, sir. Foot of York Road. Less than ten feet from the bank."

114

Mr. Sullivan looked at it a second.

"Ask Mr. Knox to come in, Basil. Stay out there until I call you."

I looked in the greatest astonishment from one to the other of the men in the room. Mr. Sullivan stood up, one hand in his pocket, the finger tips of the other beating a puzzled tattoo on his desk. Mr. Rand looked very grave, and I thought I could see a watchful flicker in his eyes.

The door opened and Franklin Knox came in. He saw the gun on the desk. From his perceptible start I thought he hadn't quite expected this.

"You shot Daniel Sutton, did you?" Mr. Sullivan said.

"I did."

"With this gun? It's a .38 calibre."

Franklin looked at it closer.

"That's the gun," he said.

"After you shot Mr. Sutton with this gun, you threw it in the river?"

"That's right."

"Where?"

"What do you mean?"

"I mean where did you go to the river to throw the gun in?"

He paused only an instant.

"I went down King Charles Street," he said.

Mr. Sullivan sat down and drew his chair forward.

"You threw this gun in the river from the foot of King Charles Street?"

"Yes," said Franklin shortly.

"That's all. Will you wait in the other room."

Franklin disappeared. Mr. Sullivan looked at Mr. Rand, whose face was almost as puzzled as my own.

"In other words, Mrs. Niles," Mr. Sullivan said, turning to me, "Franklin Knox, knowing that Thorn Carter went to your house, through the King Charles Street Gate at 2:15 this morning, assumes that before she went to your house she went down King Charles Street and threw the weapon in the river."

I started. He interpreted my surprise again.

"How do I know Thorn went through the King Charles Street gate?"

I flushed in annoyance at being so transparent.

"You omitted to tell me, and I haven't seen Thorn Carter. Well, I was told by Colonel Arbuthnot-Howe."

I stared again in amazement.

"He believes, Mrs. Niles, that the only way to clear Thorn Carter is for someone to tell the truth."

What he meant was clear enough.

"In that case," I said quickly, "I mean, if the gun was found at the foot of York Road, it can't have been Thorn."

He smiled exasperatingly. "Not necessarily. However, there were other people on York Road that night."

I tried as I looked at him to define the clear implication in his voice.

"I was there," I said tentatively.

He nodded.

"Yes, Mrs. Niles. You were. And you had a companion."

"Colonel Arbuthnot-Howe?" I demanded.

Mr. Sullivan smiled, rather like a male Irish Mona Lisa.

XXIV

I couldn't quite at the moment decide whether Mr. Sullivan thought I had thrown the weapon there in front of him into Seaton River, or whether it was Colonel Arbuthnot-Howe. Both were equally preposterous. Nevertheless, my chief point was gained—or so I thought. Thorn Carter was absolved; at least suspicion was diverted from her. More than that, Mr. Sullivan knew, thanks to Colonel Arbuthnot-Howe, that she had used the King Charles Street gate. He probably knew everything else I'd told the Englishman. There was therefore no further point in my not telling him everything I knew. As a matter of fact, it turned out that Mr. Sullivan knew a great deal that I didn't know he knew at all. Which, after all, is his job, and I suppose explains why he's been a successful State's Attorney for twenty years.

"Perhaps, Mrs. Niles," he said, taking the idea out of my mind before I'd expressed it, "you could make things much clearer by telling me exactly what happened, as far as you yourself know it, last night. We'll just forget everything you've said before and begin all over again."

The implication rather nettled me. As a matter of fact I'd merely left out things, I hadn't put any in. Nevertheless I began. I told him about hearing a click and seeing Reverdy come out of the King Charles gate at 1.00 o'clock. I told how he had stopped outside the gate under the lamp, and appeared to be counting money. I described Thorn's arrival at 2.15 and our talk. Mr. Sullivan seemed a little annoyed when I told him that the gate was locked when we went back. He seemed, however, to believe me readily enough when I told about my finding the note under the street lamp, stuffing it into my pocket and forgetting it in the extraordinary events that followed.

"And that's all," I ended, "that I didn't tell you before."

He gave me a rather sourish smile.

"Enough to make a whale of a difference, you'll have to admit. Eh, Mr. Rand?"

Mr. Rand nodded pontifically. He seemed to me either to be vastly indifferent about the whole business, all of a sudden, or to be mulling it over, examining facets that were invisible to me. Maybe he was thinking of Franklin Knox, still cooling his heels in the anteroom. I'd thought Mr. Sullivan had forgotten him until he remarked in an aside to Mr. Rand that a little solitary would be good for the young fellow.

"I think we'd better have a little chat with Reverdy?" Mr. Sullivan said.

A lank shadow on the frosted glass preceded Reverdy in. He was a very unhappy Negro, resplendent in his grey flannels, frock coat and red tie pin. He had added to them a pink shirt and a celluloid collar that had enough finger prints on it to start a rogues' gallery.

He bowed to each of us.

"Sit down, Hawkins," Mr. Sullivan ordered. Reverdy sat gingerly on the corner of a chair.

"Reverdy!" said Mr. Sullivan, regarding the colored lawyer with the most benevolent friendliness. "You've been trying to sell Aunt Charlotte's cabin to Mr. Sutton."

"Yassuh. Ah mean No suh," replied Reverdy hastily. "Ah's only actin' as her agent."

"As Aunt Charlotte's agent, Reverdy?"

"Yessuh."

"Sure you're not acting as somebody else's agent, Reverdy?"

Reverdy was palpably nonplussed. He looked from one to the other of us. He moistened his thick dry lips and swallowed very much as a chicken does in swallowing a crust of bread.

Mr. Sullivan's tone became still more confiding.

"Now look here, Reverdy. We don't want to have to put you in jail for being implicated in this business. But there's trouble about it. All we want to know is what you were doing in the grounds of Seaton Hall last night. Why you came out the King Charles Street gate, and what you've done with the money given you. Of course, Reverdy, you know you don't

117

have to explain this. You know enough about the law to know that if you don't, I'll have to put you downstairs on a charge of murder—accessory before the fact."

Reverdy turned the color of a charred oak log covered with a thin film of greyish ash. He was badly frightened. He moistened his lips; his ludicrous top hat turned round and round in his long hands.

"'Deed an' Ah'll tell you Mistuh Sullivan. All Ah knows 'bout it. Mistuh Fenton ask me to get Aunt Charlotte to sell that the' place."

He began as if the idea had never occurred to anyone before.

"An' Ah did. An' Ah went see Mistuh Sutton, an' he done say he'll pay $25,000 for that place. Then that evenin' Mistah Fenton he phone to me an' he say, it's all off. An' Ah says No suh, it ain' all off noways. Then we has some talk, and Mistuh Fenton he done agree to pay me mah commission. Mah commission was all Ah wants. If Ah'll let it go and tell Aunt Charlotte not to sell that place."

"I see, Reverdy. But you decided you'd go ahead, eh?"

"No *suh*, no *suh!* Nothin' of the sort, suh. Ah said Ah didn' see mah way cleah. So Mistuh Fenton he get real mad. He says Ah'm to come to King Charles gate that night at twelve o'clock, he wants talk with me. Ah didn' like it much, but ah goes."

Mr. Sullivan understood perfectly. Somewhat boiled down, it seemed from Reverdy's statement, which none of us dreamed of questioning, that Wally had met Reverdy and paid hin his "commission" and Reverdy had thereupon gone. He had no idea why Wally had changed his mind. Remembering Wally's long talks with Mr. Baca after dinner, and Bill's remark about his having declined the Ranch of the Spring of the Holy Ghost, I began to have a very definite notion why Wally had changed his mind.

Mr. Sullivan was finally convinced that Reverdy was merely the victim of his own cupidity and let him go.

"What do you think of that, now, Mrs. Niles?"

"I think," I said, "that Mr. Sutton knew Wally was behind the business of the service station, Mr. Sullivan."

I told him about my meeting Mr. Sutton at Aunt Charlotte's the last evening.

"I wish you'd told me that before," he said seriously.

"Mr. Sullivan," I said.

"Yes, Mrs. Niles?"

"I think that if you'd ask Franklin Knox to come in, and

tell him that you don't think Thorn had anything to do with her uncle's death, he'll tell you what he knows."

His eyes narrowed reflectively.

"But what if I *do* think she had something to do with it?"

"That's preposterous, Sullivan," Mr. Rand observed. "Anyone who knows that girl knows it's absurd."

"The income from three millions is a lot of money, Mr. Rand."

"Not enough, Sullivan."

"In any case," I put in, "if Thorn Carter had done it, she wouldn't have taken that revolver way down York Road and thrown it in the river."

"Mrs. Niles is right, Sullivan," Mr. Rand said. "That was done either by some one who is simple and logical, and did just the plainest and simplest thing to do, or it was done by a very subtle person, who did it that way to make people think it was done by someone who is simple and logical. And Thorn Carter is neither simple on the one hand nor subtle on the other."

Mr. Sullivan chewed his lower lip, soberly meditating this bit of wisdom. He nodded suddenly.

"Let's have the young fellow in," he said briefly.

"And in the meantime, if you don't mind," I put in, "I've got to get along."

Mr. Sullivan bowed and held the door open for me.

"May I tell my husband that he's not in immediate danger of having his wife in jail for murder?" I inquired meekly.

"I'll have to have notice of that question, Mrs. Niles."

Thus neatly evaded, I went out into the anteroom. Franklin was gulping down a paper cup of water from the cooler. From the number of crushed cups on the floor around the waste basket I gathered he'd consumed great quantities of the State's spring water. I felt he needed some encouragement, so when I passed him I said, "Don't be a complete ass, Franklin. Good-bye."

It was considerably after six o'clock, and the loungers in Court House Circle had separated an hour for supper. I turned from the Circle, with its pleasant mottled stockade of sycamore trees, down past St. Margaret's Church to York Road. The campus was deserted. All the students were in the dining hall. Somebody's radio was presenting a crooner to the empty street. As I reached my house the familiar figure of Dr. Knox came down the steps. Another man was with him.

"Good evening, Martha. I want you to meet Mr. Brice.

119

I've just seen your husband, and the two of you are coming to the house for dinner this evening."

I thought of the tense white-lipped young man I'd left in the State's Attorney's office.

"That's nice," I said. "Oh, by the way. I just saw Franklin."

"Yes?" said Dr. Knox. He hesitated only a moment. "What's he doing?"

"He's all right. They've found the gun, and I think I'm finally going to be able to convince Franklin that Thorn didn't do it."

He nodded. "Good," he said, with his old gentle urbanity. "We'll see you at seven, then. Good-bye."

"Good-bye."

Mr. Brice and I bowed and I went in the house.

XXV

We had dinner at Dr. Knox's that evening. Mr. Brice turned out to be an entertaining young man of twenty-eight or thereabouts, who came to be a considerable factor, as it turned out, in our lives. Mr. Rand and Franklin made up the rest of the party. Franklin looked much less harassed. I gathered that the interview with the State's Attorney had cleared things up considerably. He and Mr. Rand left early and I went as far as my house with them, leaving Ben to smoke a pipe with Dr. Knox and his guest and to talk interminably about the college.

I could understand Franklin's longing—so near the surface in his eyes—to get to Thorn, and I could understand Mr. Rand's need to get back to Seaton Hall: he had something to say to Mr. Wally. I suppose as a matter of fact I could even understand Ben's desire to smoke a pipe and discuss the college, so simple-minded is the academic soul. As for myself, my one desire was to go to bed and go fast asleep. I sent the sleepy student who stays with the children while we're out home with his unopened History of Philosophy, and I retired.

I was waked the next morning by the always startling jangle of the telephone, just as Lillie came in with my breakfast. She set my tray down and handed me the phone.

It was Susan Atwood. And it was probably the first time in her life that Susan was up before ten.

"Hello, Martha!" she fairly gurgled.

120

"What's the matter?" I said. "Are you ill?"

"No, Martha. But you've got to come over. I've got a secret to tell you."

I've been the recipient of many of Susan's secrets, all of which have been totally uninspiring.

"If it won't keep you'd better tell me now, unless you're coming over here. Because I'm not up. I've not had my breakfast, and I'm not coming near your place for at least two hours."

"Then I'll tell you. You won't breathe a word of it? Promise, hope to die?"

I repeated the pledge solemnly.

"You're not being serious, Martha!"

"Perfectly serious, Sue. What is it? My breakfast's getting cold."

"Well, then—I'm eloping!"

"Oh yes," I said, not very much surprised at anything Susan said—or did.

"*Eloping*, darling."

"Who with, or is that part of the secret? Or do you know?"

"It's all a secret, Martha. With Sebastien!"

"*Susan*—you're not!" I cried, almost upsetting my tray.

"I am too. I'm going this evening."

I didn't say anything. I couldn't think of anything to say. I'm very fond of Susan, and the idea of her running off with a man she'd known two days was unthinkable. My silence became ominous, I imagine, at the other end of the wire.

"What's the matter, Martha?" asked a small wistful voice.

"Nothing, darling. I'm surprised, that's all."

"You won't tell anybody?"

"Of course I won't. But listen—will you do something for me?"

"Surely."

"Don't go until we've talked it over. Promise?"

"That's a go. Bye-bye, Martha."

I put back the phone and sat staring at my coffee cup. It was silly of me. There wasn't any reason that Susan shouldn't marry Sebastien Baca if she chose; and apparently she did. I knew nothing against him, and I'd trust Susan's instincts anywhere. She must have recognized him as the right sort or she wouldn't have been so instantly drawn to him. More than that, I'm convinced that people—women as well as men—must take life as it comes to them. If it came to Susan this way, that was just part of it. Susan is too pure metal to be hurt, I thought. Then I thought of a gold cup I'd seen Dr. Myerfrank dig up in Tuscany. It was tarnished—and I didn't want Susan tarnished, even if she could be polished up again like the Tuscan cup.

I thought about Sebastien Baca while I bathed and dressed. The idea, never very far from my mind, that he knew Colonel Arbuthnot-Howe, kept cropping persistently up to plague me. Why had he looked so startled at lunch when the Englishman's name was mentioned? Why had he stiffened when Miss Carter asked Colonel Arbuthnot-Howe if he'd been in Mexico? Why, to take another point, had Colonel Arbuthnot-Howe asked me to find out how sick he was that morning?

Then a new crop of questions. Was it true that he'd consulted Mr. Sutton on the matter of the ranch? Was it true that he didn't know Mr. Sutton had been murdered? Or was he putting on an act for the benefit of Mrs. Niles, friend of the family? Why had he and Wally been so thick before the swimming party, when Wally had been so obviously rude to him at lunch? Why had Wally been so absolutely "sunk" when we met the two of them sitting on a marble bench in the linden avenue on our way to the river? Why had Mr. Baca been so entirely debonair?

Gradually I came to the swimming party itself. What was the meaning of Sebastien Baca's accident? Was it anything more than that? What had Colonel Arbuthnot-Howe meant by what he said about a bruise on the Mexican's face? Why was Wally so upset? I remembered now that even Dan had seemed to notice that something was wrong. Mr. Baca was a marvellous swimmer; so was Wally. For an instant I closed my eyes. The picture of Wally's hag-ridden face in the clear moonlight, as Arbuthnot-Howe mentioned that bruised face, flashed across my mind. I decided I had to talk with Susan.

Lafayette opened the door for me.

"Mornin' Miss. How *is* you, Miss?"

"Good morning, Lafayette. I'm well. How're you?"

"Ah' m well Miss. It's a nice day."

"That's good, Lafayette. It *is* a nice day."

"How's the doctor, Miss, and them children?"

"They're all right, Lafayette. Is anybody down?"

"That's good, Miss. Yas'm, Miss Susan's outside and so's Mistah Bill. Mistah Nathan's in the liberry talkin' to Mistah Sullivan."

"Thanks, Lafayette," I said. "I'll go outside."

I went through the hall and out on the wide verandah. Seaton's long green velvet carpet stretched softly down to the glistening dancing river. Everything was gorgeously vital

122

and alive. A cardinal lighted on the grass like a single drop of blood.

"Hello," said a gloomy voice at my side.

I turned around. It was Bill, lying on his spine in a grass chair, his long legs stretched uselessly in front of him. He was the very picture of dejection.

"Hello!" I said. "What's the matter with you?"

"Nothing."

"Splendid. Where's Susan?"

He hunched himself up with a savage jerk and threw his cigarette violently on the flags.

"Down in the orangery talking to that damn Spaniard."

I looked placidly at him.

"Sebastien," he added, with a mocking imitation of Susan.

"I see," I said.

"Do you know what she did, Martha?" he demanded, running his hand through his crisp curly hair.

"Haven't the faintest."

"She went in there—in the library—and got out a picture of some beastly saint, all stuck full of arrows, and hung the damn thing up in her room. She said it was St. Sebastien."

"So it was if it was all full of arrows," I said peaceably. "He's a very respectable saint, as you'd know if you knew anything at all about saints."

"So *she* said. I told her if she didn't stop following him around like a puppy I'd fill him full of worse than arrows. It's disgusting."

He hunched forward, staring out down the green terraces, miserably but righteously indignant.

"Why so?" I inquired.

"Look here, Martha," he said. "You're not going to sit here and see her throw herself away at that . . . that . . ."

"That what?"

"That Mexican?"

"What's the matter with him, Bill?"

He stared at me as if I'd lost my mind. Then he shrugged his shoulders.

"Oh, nothing, I guess," he admitted after a moment. "Only I . . . I don't like it. I guess that's all."

He jumped up and did a couple of absurd turns up and down the verandah.

"Then do something about it," I said. "Don't sit here like an idiot."

With that sage bit of advice I went inside and upstairs to Thorn's room. She was in front of her dressing table, singing that fish gotta swim and birds gotta fly. I understood the conclusion to be that she intended to love Franklin until she died.

"Oh, my dear!" she said. She got up, came over to me and threw her arms around my neck. "He didn't do it. He didn't do it."

"All right," I said. "I didn't think he did."

"I was so afraid," she went on, "because when I went downstairs I knew it was Franklin by the light switch. I knew it, and I was frightened. I wanted to get over to you without having to speak to him, so I wouldn't *know* it was him."

"But you did know it," I said, sitting down in the window seat.

"I knew it inside of me, but I hadn't seen him. I just sensed him. If I'd seen him or spoken to him, or he'd said 'It's Franklin,' then I'd have had to tell Mr. Sullivan—in fairness to Uncle Dan."

I passed over that. She sat down beside me, and absently both our gazes roamed through the window; and both of us caught the flash of Susan's yellow head in the orangery. Sebastien Baca was beside her.

"I wonder how poor Bill's taking it," said Thorn, shaking her head dreamily.

"Why?"

"Oh, you know it's always been taken for granted that Bill and Susan would marry. Even Uncle Dan thought so. Bill did too. Now she's upset the apple cart."

"Definitely?"

"Perhaps not definitely. Definitely enough so that Dan, who's chiefly noted for minding his own business, as well as asked Aunt Mildred to ask Baca to leave."

I looked at her in surprise.

"Aunt Mildred asked Mr. Rand, and he said he'd ask Mr. Sullivan."

No wonder, I thought, if that's the case, that young Sue decided to go along. I was a little annoyed at Thorn. After what she'd been through the last week she seemed rather callous about Susan's little affair.

"Well," I said, "what are you going to do now? Sit in your ivory tower, or come out of it?"

She smiled wanly. Her desperate struggle of the day before had left her smooth eggshell cheeks the transparent waxiness of a white magnolia petal.

"I've come out already," she said. "I had an hour's chat with Mr. Sullivan. I gathered that either Franklin or Wally, or you or I, did it. Bill was here with us—as chaperon. He

124

came out of the dumps long enough to suggest we play a foursome to decide."

"I thought Mr. Sullivan had decided you and Franklin and I were out of it?"

"I thought he'd decided absolutely nothing," Thorn said. "But it doesn't matter. I know I didn't do it, and I know you didn't, and I know Franklin didn't. As for Wally, it's just the sort of trick I'd expect from him."

We lapsed into silence. I was thinking about Susan, and I suppose Thorn was thinking fuzzy indefinable things the way one does. We heard a sound below of someone walking on the gravel path, and looked down. It was young Basil the state policeman. We watched him make his way down the path, disappearing under the feathery maze of a pink magnolia. He reappeared again in the entrance to the orangery. Thorn and I looked at each other, then back at him. Susan and Sebastien Baca rose to their feet. I saw the Mexican turn and bow to Susan. Then he and young Basil started back to the house together. Thorn and I looked silently at one another.

XXVI

While Thorn and I were still discussing the probabilities of Mr. Baca's summons, Miss Carter's maid appeared with the news that her aunt was not well and would like to see her. It seemed that from the day of Daniel Sutton's death Miss Carter had spent practically all of her time in her room. It was Thorn's belief that while he was alive she hadn't dared to have even a headache, and that she had now, in a new freedom, abandoned herself to the vapours like any eighteenth century Seaton.

We separated in the hall.

"I'm going to see Susan," I said.

"See if you can get her to give up her Aztec prince," Thorn called after me.

"I've got more sense than that."

When I was half-way down the stairs I saw the library door open and Susan's Aztec prince come out, his urbanity more than a little ruffled.

"Hello," I said. "How are you by now?"

He bowed rigidly.

"Good morning," he said in his precise English. "I am

125

very well, thank you so much. Do you think I might speak with you for a moment?"

"Surely," I said. I joined him at the foot of the stairs and we went into the front drawing room and sat down, near the side window. I thought it was rather a shame to keep him from Susan.

"I want to talk with you, Mrs. Niles," he said, "because you are the only one here who seems in the least friendly towards me."

"Miss Atwood?"

He smiled, but the smile disappeared at once.

"But this other thing," he said with a frown. "It seems there is some belief here that I am connected with Mr. Fenton—or that he is connected with me in my project for the ranch."

"Isn't he?"

"No, no, no, senora . . . Mrs. Niles." He shrugged, and raised the palms of his hands in absolute despair at the idea.

"I have never seen Mr. Fenton before I came here."

"Really?"

"Really."

His response was very emphatic.

"I came here, as I told you, to try to buy El rancho del Ojo del Espiritu Santo from Mr. Sutton. My fathers owned it, they were great landholders. They sold it to Senator Centrone, who left the rancho to his widow. Mr. Sutton paid her twenty-five cents the acre—there are two hundred fifty thousand acres—and he established a fund for her. I offered him one dollar the acre. You see, I am an engineer, and I have backers with much money, a syndicate in California and Mexico. But Mr. Sutton said no. Then I explained to him how great value the land has—two hundred and fifty thousand acres with oil, oil shale, gold maybe, silver certainly, copper, lead, gypsum, antimony, zinc, galena, arsenic—they may all be there, in the greatest quantities."

"Really!" I gasped, beginning to understand now for the first time the extent of the thing.

"Yes, really. And Mr. Sutton thinks he will develop this land then, himself. He is tired of this life, he will go with me. Together we will survey the land, and form a company. We make big plans, Mrs. Niles. Then this thing . . . ah!"

He buried his head in his hands and shook it stormily.

"Then they tell me I am connected with Fenton."

"It's probably because you and he talked so much together that night," I said calmly.

"No, no!" he cried. He jumped up, and paced back and

126

forth with sparkling eyes and wild gestures. Then he sat down as abruptly, and began, with elaborated gesticulation, to tell me what had happened in his interview with Mr. Sullivan.

"The young officer said they wished to speak with me. I have already talked with Mr. Rand, but because you had said Mr. Sutton was murdered I have said nothing more than I could. I go in there. There sits Mr. Rand with telegrams, they are from Barton, the mining engineers in Los Angeles. They have investigated for him, they have found there is no doubt the Rancho del Ojo del Espiritu Santo will be worth millions."

And none of us, I thought, in our quiet Maryland hamlet, had seen further than our noses.

"Mr. Sullivan then turns to Fenton, and says, You know this. Mr. Fenton then—like you, Madam—says Really? That makes Mr. Sullivan angry. So I know that Mr. Fenton has been saying Really? for some time. Then Mr. Sullivan points his finger at Fenton and accuses him of trying to sell his Aunt Charlotte's cabin for $25,000."

I let the relationship go uncontested. "What then?" I asked.

"He was not comfortable. He—what is it you say?—he swaggered. He said, Yes, he did. The old man had pots of money and did nothing for him. He would make $15,000 which he needed. His uncle would have the cabin, which he wanted. His Aunt Charlotte would have $9,000, and somebody would have $1,000. He admitted this all."

"What did Mr. Sullivan say?"

The slim elegant shoulders shrugged eloquently.

"He said, 'Why did you suddenly give up the idea?' "

"What did Wally say?"

"Mrs. Niles," he said, looking at me severely, "you are as bad as Susan. If you will give me a chance I will tell you."

I felt that perhaps he wouldn't be a bad husband for Susan after all.

"Fenton said he had decided it was not worth the trouble. And that was all, not another thing could they get out of him. Then he suggested that Fenton talked to me, or I to Fenton, and I persuaded him to go in the project of the Rancho with me, and Oh! I don't know what else! He brought out these telegrams showing the Rancho to be valuable. And he demanded an explanation from Fenton."

"Which Fenton declined to give."

"Yes," Mr. Baca nodded. "He then accused Fenton of a murderous attack on my life, while we were swimming, to get the whole thing for himself!"

127

He looked at me with a smile.

"Well?" I said.

"Oh, it is so absurd. No, no, it was nothing. There is no connection."

"It must have been something. You were almost drowned and something or someone struck you."

"You are fanciful, Mrs. Niles. No, no. I am a mining engineer. I have no interest in violence. My one desire is to do my business and return to my wife."

I can't remember that I was ever before literally struck speechless. I stared at him open-mouthed, with what must have been a most ludicrously half-witted expression.

"Your what?" I said at last.

He looked puzzled.

"My wife."

I said, "Oh."

"Now this is my difficulty, Mrs. Niles. I am interested deeply—so very deeply—in the development of the rancho. I wish to know who inherits this ranch under Mr. Sutton's will. But I am not, as you see, in the position to make such inquiries myself. Indeed, Mr. Sullivan has practically accused me of opening the safe to find out for myself."

He shrugged again, in deep resignation.

"Was anything taken?" I asked perfunctorily. I wasn't at all interested in that.

"I understand nothing."

I was simply overwhelmed at the amazing audacity of the cool young man sitting next to me. It was clear that he didn't know Susan had told me their plans. The thought that this handsome olive-skinned adventurer had come to Seaton Hall to get the ranch, and failing that was taking Susan—whose private fortune is considerable—made me almost ill. Worse than that, I didn't know what to do about it.

He failed to notice my perturbation.

"Now I am leaving this afternoon. Some time soon the will must be read. If I leave you my card, will you let me know to whom the ranch goes, so that I can open negotiations with him? Am I asking too much, Mrs. Niles?"

"Not at all, Mr. Baca," I said, hurriedly taking the card. I thought it might be useful some day. "Not at all."

"Of course," he went on with a shrug, "I may not be allowed to go this afternoon. I may be held by Mr. Sullivan."

I got up.

"I've got to go down and see Susan," I said pointedly. He didn't turn a hair. I thought I'd never seen a more accomplished villain.

We went out of the room together. Colonel Arbuthnot-Howe was in the hall talking to Dan. The Mexican joined them, and after speaking to them I went on outside, glad to get a breath of fresh air and anxious to speak to Susan.

She was in the orangery practising chip shots with a mashie niblick.

"I thought you'd been arrested or something," she said. "What's the matter? You look like you'd seen poor Tim's ghost."

"I haven't. But I want to talk to you, young woman. Put that wretched club away and sit down here."

"I suppose I oughtn't to be doing anything so frivolous," she said repentantly. "I didn't think anybody'd see me . . . and anyway, Martha, I don't feel a bit sad. Not really."

I was afraid she would in a minute. She sat down and I told her in a very few words what I had to say.

She sat there, digging at the lawn with the toe of the club. I thought for a while that I could have saved myself my pains. She seemed entirely unmoved. I found it hard to understand her. Pretty soon, however, I saw a great bright tear trembling on her long curling lashes. It coursed slowly down her smooth tanned cheek. Another followed, and another. Susan was crying. Suddenly she broke into sobs, and between them managed to tell me a pathetic little story that was the quintessence of tragedy for her small life.

I left her after a few minutes and went back towards the house. Lafayette was making his way painfully down the terrace steps. He saw me and stopped.

"Mistah Nathan done huntin' for you, Miss," he said, shaking his head ominously. "They wants to talk to you in the liberry."

"Thanks, Lafayette. I'll go right along."

XXVII

Mr. Rand was seated in a wing chair drawn up to the long mahogany table. He had the pile of telegrams that I'd heard about so often in front of him. He looked rather more pontifical than ever. His heavy face was deadly serious.

Mr. Sullivan appeared to be still smouldering from his interview with Wally. He was pacing up and down in front of the fireplace, emitting occasional hostile snorts.

"Sit down, Mrs. Niles," said Mr. Rand.

My heart was in my shoes as I did so.

"Mrs. Niles," he said with alarming gentleness, "did your husband know, or have any way of knowing, that Mr. Sutton intended withdrawing the trust fund for that chair of Anthropology?"

"No, Mr. Rand. Not only that. He didn't know—and so far as I know, unless someone else told him, he doesn't yet know—that there is such a fund."

Mr. Sullivan spoke up.

"He does know it," he said shortly. "Dr. Knox told him some time ago. I asked him why he hadn't told you. He said that Sutton changed his mind so often he didn't want to have you disappointed."

I found myself growing unaccountably angry.

"Well?" I said.

"I'm suggesting, Mrs. Niles," he snapped, "that both you and your husband knew you were, in the event of Mr. Sutton's death, to get most of the income on $200,000. And that your husband, having quarrelled with Mr. Sutton, realized that you were about to lose that income."

I stood up, perfectly furious. Mr. Rand said nothing.

"Have you any notion what my husband and Mr. Sutton quarrelled about?" I asked.

"No. Mr. Niles wouldn't discuss it. He said it was entirely unimportant."

"Then I'll tell you what it was. It was about which the college needed more, a chemistry laboratory or an athletic bowl. My husband didn't even know it was a quarrel, until Dr. Knox told him about it yesterday. More than that, the discussion didn't take place until they had finished three rubbers of bridge the night of the swimming party."

Mr. Sullivan was silent for a moment.

"Have you ever seen this gun before?" he asked suddenly, bringing the .38 revolver out from a drawer in the table.

"I saw it yesterday on your desk, if that's the one."

"Not before?"

"Never."

"It doesn't belong to Professor Niles?"

"It certainly doesn't."

"Do you know who it does belong to?"

"No, I don't. I just told you I'd never seen it before."

He put it back in the drawer and resumed his pacing.

"Please sit down, Mrs. Niles," said Mr. Rand.

I sat down again, and so did Mr. Sullivan.

"Mrs. Niles," he said, "I want you to realize your husband's position."

"I don't see that he's got one," I returned. "You have in this house two perfect strangers, each here, as far as I can see, with the definite purpose of getting land of great value that belonged to Mr. Sutton. Neither of them has a ghost of an alibi. You even have the evidence of Franklin Knox that one or both of them were up that night around two o'clock. Instead of finding out what they were up to, you trump up an absurd excuse for involving first Thorn Carter, then me, then my husband. It's preposterous."

Mr. Sullivan looked a little surprised at my outburst, and so did Mr. Rand. They looked at each other. Then Mr. Sullivan said, "We are investigating Mr. Sutton's two guests, Mrs. Niles. Will you tell me about your conversation yesterday with Colonel Arbuthnot-Howe?"

"What do you mean?" I asked.

"He came to me in the afternoon, after you'd gone, and said you were disturbed about Thorn Carter, but .that he felt the best policy was to put all cards on the table. I agreed. He said you didn't, and for that reason he'd decided, in Miss Thorn's interest, to tell me what you'd told him."

"I see," I said acidly. "Did he tell you anything else?"

"What do you mean?" said Mr. Rand steadily.

"Did he tell you that he said he was sleeping quietly in Wally's room on the second floor from a little after one until he heard me scream?"

Mr. Sullivan nodded questioningly.

"Did Thorn tell you that when she heard something at two o'clock she went in Wally's room and found it empty?"

Mr. Sullivan leaned forward with interest.

"Are you sure of that?"

"Yes. And did Colonel Arbuthnot-Howe tell you why, when he came downstairs ar four o'clock, he was dressed in pajamas and a dressing gown—and had on rubber soled shoes instead of bedroom slippers?"

They were listening intently.

"More than that. When Wally Fenton announced at lunch that Colonel Arbuthnot-Howe was coming here I happened to glance at Mr. Baca. He looked almost stunned. At dinner when Miss Carter asked Colonel Arbuthnot-Howe if he'd been in Mexico, Mr. Baca straightened up like a ramrod. Yet Colonel Arbuthnot-Howe says he didn't know him. Mr. Baca certainly knows Colonel Arbuthnot-Howe."

I stopped for breath, and as I did so I realized that in my fury, and my desire to protect Ben, I'd made some rather dangerous accusations.

"I accused him of being a detective," I said more calmly.

131

Mr. Rand shot a lightning glance at me. I got the impression that he wished I'd be a little more discreet.

"What did he say to that?" Mr. Sullivan asked.

"He smiled."

Mr. Rand cleared his throat.

"I think it's dangerous," he said slowly, "to implicate a person of Arbuthnot-Howe's standing in an affair of this sort. He is after all a colonel in the British army. I know his uncle and respect him highly. He's here with a definite mission—he's told all of you about that, Mrs. Niles. If he has any other mission, it seems to fall in your line, Sullivan."

I thought it was clear that Mr. Rand knew more than we did—at least more than I did. Was Mr. Baca playing with fire, after all?

"At any rate, Mr. Sullivan," I said with determination, "two things are true. One is that someone in the lodge released the latch so we could open the gate night before last. The other is that somebody was in this room when we came through the hall."

"I'm aware of that, Mrs. Niles," he said shortly. "If you see Miss Thorn Carter will you ask her to come in here?"

I accepted my dismissal gratefully, and went out into the hall and straight into the arms, as it were, of Colonel Arbuthnot-Howe. My eyes met his twinkling steely grey ones, wrinkling a little at the corners, rather amused, I thought, at my discomfiture. It must have been pretty obvious.

I must admit that I was very much ashamed of myself. I had someway in the last half hour changed my mental picture of him. To see him now absolutely unchanged, just as fine-looking, as keenly intelligent and alert and kindly as ever, was a shock to me.

"I've just done you in frightfully," I said sheepishly.

He grinned broadly.

"How, Mrs. Niles?"

"I got angry at Mr. Sullivan for accusing my husband of shooting Mr. Sutton, and I told him you weren't in your room the other night."

He raised his eyebrows in a quizzical mock alarm.

"What's that? and how did you know it?" he demanded amiably.

"Thorn went in there to get Wally up, and the room was empty. Then you told me you and Wally had changed rooms. It was all very simple."

"It just goes to show, Mrs. Niles," he replied, shaking his head solemnly. "And you let me put my foot in it without saying a word. Tut tut! Is that friendly?"

"I did say a word, I said 'Oh.' Well, then I told Mr. Sullivan that you had on rubber-soled shoes, and that Mr. Baca knows you if you don't know him."

He smiled again. Then his sun-bronzed face became very serious.

"I should have had more respect for your powers of observation, Mrs. Niles," he said soberly.

"I'm sorry if I've been a nuisance," I said.

"Oh not at all."

"Then I'll see you later. I've got to get Thorn now. Mr. Sullivan is going to grill her again."

"Cheerio," he said. I went upstairs to find Thorn.

I had a job of work—as Lillie says—to do for Susan at Seaton Hall that afternoon. It was a little after two o'clock when I came down my garden walk, just in time to see Wally's blue roadster tearing out of York Road into the Baltimore pike.

The Suttons had finished lunch. By discreet investigation I discovered that the two girls and Miss Carter were upstairs, Dan was with Mr. Rand in the library, Mr. Baca was (so Bill said) in the guest wing packing, and Bill in complete dejection still was playing solitaire in the back drawing room.

"This whole place is cockeyed," he said, shoving back the bridge table and turning a pair of troubled brown eyes to me.

"What's the matter with it?"

I offered him a cigarette. He took it with entirely no interest in whether he lived or died, smoked or didn't smoke.

"Oh, everything. You know, it's funny, Martha, but four days ago I was just thinking all of a sudden that we're all pretty happy here."

He offered that thought rather tentatively, with a glance at me. I don't suppose Bill had ever thought of, much less discussed, the problem of human happiness before. Parlor philosophy wasn't his line, decidedly. He didn't know now quite how to handle it.

"I mean, you know, even with Dad being hard to get on with and everything. . . . Then suddenly everything just went to pieces."

"And you're not happy now?"

"I guess not."

"Well," I said, getting up. "I've got to get along. I'm helping Susan pack."

He jumped as if he had got an electric shock.

"What the . . . ?" he demanded coarsely.

"Pack. Susan. Helping her," I said amiably.

133

"What do you mean? She's not going?"

"Must be, or she wouldn't be packing. Or so *I* should think."

Suddenly he flared up like a rocket.

"Is she going with that damn Mexican?"

I attempted an arch smile.

"I'll put a stop to that. Where is he?"

That was my cue.

"Where is she, is more to the point," I said calmly.

He looked at me very like a child trying to understand how the moon and the stars are so far away. Then he turned and in a second I heard him taking the steps three and four at a time. I heard a door burst open and slam shut.

My job of work for Susan was done. I sat down and finished Bill's game of solitaire.

XXVIII

I'll never forget the rest of that day as long as I live. It seemed almost as if Mr. Sutton's death—we'd quit calling it by its other name—had happened years before, and was a sort of background for what was going on instead of its motivating force.

I was just shuffling the deck for another try at my game of solitaire when Wally came in through the side door from the guest hyphen. He didn't look very well. His drawn face was almost ludicrous in contrast with his lacquered black hair and immaculate blue suit and dark tie—as if somebody had dressed a dummy and then plastered the wrong face on it.

I glanced up, smugly aware that I was very glad I wasn't in his shoes. As a matter of fact, I wondered how he had courage to stick around. I think I'd have gone and crawled in a hole somewhere.

"Have you seen Arbuthnot?" he asked.

"Not since before lunch. Why?"

"I just wondered," he said uneasily. "There's a fellow out-side from the British Embassy. I just wondered."

"He's probably upstairs."

I saw for the first time a move that would have taken the ten of hearts, which I'd just blocked the two of spades with. As I don't believe in cheating myself at solitaire I didn't go back, and consequently I finished with only six cards out. Wally still stood in the middle of the room, his face a picture of irresolution.

"I thought you were on your way to Baltimore," I said, by way of making conversation while dealing down seven cards.

"I?"

I nodded, dealing out six more.

"I saw you going into the Baltimore pike on two wheels. How long do you think it'll be before they straighten out that curve? Somebody's going to get killed there."

I dealt down five, then four, and so on, and found myself confronted with one king, no aces, and nothing else above a five spot. It was a hopeless layout and I lost interest in it.

I glanced at Wally, still standing there in the middle of the room. As far as I could see he was trying to pull his tiny black mustache to bits. Quite abruptly he turned and left the room by the French window off the garden verandah. I went back to my game, but only for a minute or so. Mr. Rand suddenly appeared in the door.

"Have you seen Arbuthnot-Howe, Mrs. Niles?"

"No," I said. "Why?"

He didn't stop to answer, but turned back at once. I heard his heavy tread going slowly up the stairs. I sat still thinking about Wally, and how oddly he was acting, and wondering what was in store for him. Mr. Sullivan suddenly stuck his head in the door.

"Have you seen Colonel Arbuthnot-Howe, Mrs. Niles?"

"No," I said. "Why?"

He didn't answer me either, unless an unintelligible snarl can be taken as an answer. Its meaning seemed to be clear enough.

With that I abandoned my solitaire and went out into the hall. It was curious how a little crowd of us gathered there all of a sudden, quite as though the dénouement of the piece were unexpectedly at hand. Dan was there when I came in, and Thorn and Franklin came in a minute or so later. Mr. Rand came downstairs looking very worried; and after a bit Bill and Susan appeared, like a radiant youth and maiden from the vales of Cyprus, holding each other's hand. Shamelessly.

No one seemed to know quite what was the matter. Then Mr. Sullivan came back, and motioned us all into the front drawing room.

"I have just got information," he said quietly, "that indicates the arrest of Colonel Arbuthnot-Howe." He wasn't in the least pompous or important, now that he might have some reason for being.

We all gasped. Susan's eyes were like blue delft saucers. And just then Mr. Baca stepped into the room. Susan didn't seem even to see him.

Mr. Sullivan put on his horn-rimmed spectacles and consulted a typed sheet of paper.

"I have Colonel Arbuthnot-Howe's dossier from the British Embassy records," he said shortly. "And I may say that he's everything he described himself as being. However, he's also a good deal more."

I remember so clearly that moment. Mr. Sullivan's slightly rasping voice, drily reading off those surprising details; Mr. Rand sitting by him, the little group sitting around the room, Mr. Baca, slim and graceful, standing by the door. And how I had been deceived in Colonel Arbuthnot-Howe! There was a good deal that wasn't relevant in that dossier; but I suppose to Mr. Sullivan's mind most of it was not only relevant but conclusive. Height six feet four, it said; broad shoulders, weight sixteen stone; eyes blue-grey; hair light brown; always sun-tanned; pleasant expression and manner. Limps slightly from wound received in action in 1916. D.S.C.; V.C. for extraordinary valor under fire. He had without question a most distinguished military record. There was one exploit at which I caught my breath quickly; it was an extraordinary feat performed in the Dardanelles, after his wound; and he had been chosen for it because he was the best swimmer in the British army. There followed in the dossier a concise list of medals, cups and championships won before the War.

I think every eye in the room was fixed for a second on Sebastien Baca. I know that mine were then lowered an instant, a tribute to a brave man.

There was the other side of the medal then. A younger son of a younger son of an old family impoverished by income tax and death duties. There was no place in post-war England for such a man; and then the adventurer—never entirely dishonorable, not always entirely reputable—wandering from Ireland to Australia to Mexico to Siberia to Africa.

Mr. Sullivan paused.

"You can tell us, I understand, about Colonel Arbuthnot-Howe in Mexico?" he said.

Mr. Baca shook his head.

"Very little, I'm afraid. I knew him in Mexico City only as an adventurer and a gambler, and as a very charming man received in the best society. But when in New Mexico I came across him again. He was working, I was told, with a syndicate formed of men like himself, trying to get control of a great section of land."

He smiled with a flash of white teeth, and shrugged deprecatingly.

"I did not know how determined they were, until Colonel Arbuthnot-Howe—what is it, Bill Sutton, you said to me if I did not leave Miss Susan alone—smashed me in the jaw, when we were swimming. You see, I had finished my arrangement with Mr. Sutton. The Colonel was a little too late. Still, if he could incapacitate me, he might make a deal. He did not know how far that I had got with Mr. Sutton."

"He was trying to drown you?" Thorn asked abruptly.

The eyebrows, the hands, the slim shoulders raised together.

"But I don't know. I do not think so. It was an intimidation. Or let us think so. But," he added with an engaging smile, "I do not think Colonel Arbuthnot-Howe would have hesitated to drown me, if it had seemed necessary."

Mr. Sullivan glanced down at the typed sheet in front of him.

"There is one other point to clear up," he said, and left the room followed by Mr. Rand. The rest of us gathered in two little knots and talked, I suppose incoherently, about it.

"I hope they don't find him," Thorn said suddenly.

Susan smiled suddenly at Mr. Baca.

"I don't think they will," she said. "Sebastien and I helped him put his bag in Wally's car. He said he'd leave it at the Calvert Street garage in Baltimore."

Mr. Baca smiled amiably.

"And, on another matter, I believe I may congratulate you, sir?" He bowed to Bill, and held out his hand.

Bill shook it heartily, looking rather flustered.

Mr. Baca turned to Susan and bowed again.

"Consider me always at your service, Señorita," he said, with a smile that had perhaps the faintest trace of good-humored mockery in it.

Susan blushed a little more than was becoming.

"Well, I had to," she said stoutly. "I couldn't have Bill going on thinking I was his sister forever. That's what happened to Aunt Mildred."

Mr. Sullivan returned.

"I'd like all of you to know that at least for the time being you're at liberty. Mr. Fenton has cleared up several points. He was helping Colonel Arbuthnot-Howe to get hold of this ranch land, which as a matter of fact Mr. Sutton had once

137

offered him, if he'd give up the stock market and go out and raise cattle on it."

Susan sniggered audibly. Dan and Thorn glared at her; Bill glared at them.

"Fenton did not know Mr. Baca's arrangements with his uncle, until Mr. Baca himself told him something of them. He at once reported to Colonel Arbuthnot-Howe, who decided to investigate for himself. Fenton has told me that at about twenty minutes of two that morning Arbuthnot-Howe waked him up, told him that Sutton was dead and that Tim Healy was dead, and forced him to come downstairs. Arbuthnot-Howe sent him to the lodge to see that no one went out, or to find out who tried to get out. Fenton had a matter of his own to settle. He went down to lock the King Charles Street gate, which he'd left open for Reverdy Hawkins. He was almost there when Miss Thorn Carter ran past him on her way to meet Franklin Knox. Bill Sutton had himself unlocked the gate for Thorn Carter, just after he had helped bring Mr. Baca to the house."

I thought, glancing around the room, that the whole family looked uncomfortably like a pack of unsuccessful conspirators.

"Fenton saw Thorn Carter go through the gate. He locked it and came back to the lodge. What he had in mind I'm not sure. It was he who pressed the control to admit Thorn Carter and Mrs. Niles, who of course thought it was Tim Healy letting them in."

I felt this to be a personal vindication, but prematurely, as I discovered later.

"It was undoubtedly Colonel Arbuthnot-Howe who was in the library. What he was doing with the safe is hard to say. Perhaps he was trying to find some record of Mr. Baca's arrangement with Mr. Sutton. At any rate, it was certainly he whom Mrs. Niles heard in the back drawing room."

He paused, a heavy frown on his brow.

"Colonel Arbuthnot-Howe was on York Road late that night. The revolver that shot Mr. Sutton was found in the river at the foot of York Road. He was also the first to find Mr. Sutton's body. I have a warrant out for his arrest. That is all."

There was a silence. Then Susan said in her firm, confident, rather defiant young voice, "I'm sorry, Mr. Sullivan, but *I* don't believe Colonel Arbuthnot-Howe killed Uncle Dan."

Mr. Sullivan looked at her through his spectacles. Then he took them off and looked at her.

"Oh," he said. "You don't?"

He picked up his papers and went out of the room. The rest of us sat around talking with some excitement about it, demanding further information of Mr. Baca, and finding out from Franklin what the legal aspects of the case were.

"Isn't Wally the swell guy," Bill remarked suddenly, and we agreed. That was almost the only comment the Suttons ever made about their cousin. The day he left Susan stood in the door and with one palm airily whisked some imaginary dust from the other.

"The blue-eyed boy is gone," she said. "And that, said John, is that."

XXIX

Several weeks slipped by in Landover. The college term was nearing an end. Most of us were getting ready to go away, and the rest were settling down for the long hot sleepy months until the college opened again in September. The college itself was a hive of activity. Most of the boys were straining to be off. The seniors roamed around with that sick look in their eyes that comes to every boy when he's leaving for the final time. The old college isn't so deadly a grind as it's been pretended, and most of the faculty aren't such bad eggs when you get down to it.

It's the familiar soul-sickness of the senior. I've listened to six generations of them at Landover. For each of them the experience is as unique and bewildering as is all human experience.

Mr. Rand was down from New York.

Suddenly Commencement was on us. Meeting parents oddly grateful that this their child had come at last to wear his cap and gown, and all the rest of it that makes each commencement an old story but a constantly new one, and never lets a college town get very old or un-understanding.

I was coming home one warm soft evening toward the end of May from a tea for the seniors at the library. I saw the familiar figure of the State's Attorney. We greeted each other cordially, but not as cordially as before the grilling days just after Mr. Sutton's death. A certain restraint marked our relations, even at the oyster supper and bridge at St. Margaret's Parish House. But this evening Mr. Sullivan was rather expansive, and I was at peace with the world.

"How do you do, Mrs. Niles," he said, stopping.

"How do you do, Mr. Sullivan. Have you heard anything of Colonel Arbuthnot-Howe?"

I suppose it was rather impolite of me, under the circumstances. One can't expect State's Attorneys to like references to men who've escaped them.

He looked at me quizzically from under his protruding grey brows. He pursed his lips. He shook his head.

"No, Mrs. Niles. No, we haven't ever found him. He parked Fenton's car in the garage and posted Miss Atwood the claim check with his love to me scribbled on the back of it. And that's the last anybody's seen of the fellow. Clever man, that."

"I suppose he is," I said.

Mr. Sullivan looked pleasantly at me.

"Do you know," he said, "I could have pushed after him harder than I did."

"You could?" I said.

"And do you know why I didn't?"

"No, Mr. Sullivan. Why?"

"Because I don't think, really, that he did it. Do you know, I don't think I'd have a case against him if I did catch him. He had no motive, Mrs. Niles. Not a ghost of one. Fenton was different; but of course he didn't have G.U. enough, if you know what I mean. There was only one other person who had the motive, and the opportunity, and the courage, Mrs. Niles. I mean a real motive. Not a sentimental false one like Thorn Carter's."

"Yes, Mr. Sullivan?"

"Yes, Mrs. Niles. Only one person with the motive, the courage, the opportunity."

He looked steadily at me, with that same calculating glance out of narrowed eyes that annoyed me so much during his investigation.

"And can you find anyone else who'd give a greater shock to poor Tim Healy, for that matter, Mrs. Niles?"

Mr. Sullivan has never actually said it, of course, in so many words; and as far as I know he's implied it only to me personally; but he still thinks I shot Daniel Sutton to save the chair of Anthropology and $8,000 a year for Ben, and that the shock of seeing me do it killed Tim Healy. Well, probably it would have, if he had seen me do such a thing.

Mr. Sullivan, encased firmly in the prejudices of his class, his profession and his locality, will never know who it was who shot Daniel Sutton. He has as little suspicion to this moment as I had then, when I talked with him as I was coming home from the tea in the library. Two people knew it then. I made a third. There will never be any more, and in the course of things, one of us at least is bound to go soon.

Commencement morning was warm, the campus was lovely with its feathery canopy of tulip poplars, maples and elms. The seats for the exercises had been arranged in front of Mascham Hall. I had shaken as much of the smell of mothballs from Ben's gown as I could. You can always tell by the odor they leave in their wake whether a professor's gown is his own or whether he rents it for the occasion.

A little before ten I went down to Aunt Charlotte's to get her and bring her over to see the young gennamen all dressed up fit to kill. It's one of her chief pleasures. I passed the great barred gate of Seaton Hall. All the Seatons had gone to Maine for the summer. I felt a little tightening in my throat, as I aways do when I go by the high wrought iron bars with the crest of the Seatons at the top.

Aunt Charlotte was ready, had been ready for hours, I imagine. She was done up in the assorted cast-off finery of fifty years of Seaton ladies. A hat not unlike my own was perched on her kerchiefed head, but it came off after a moment and we parked it under a box bush until after the ceremony. I deposited her in a chair especially placed for her, at some distance from the parents and other spectators, and went to look for some of my own friends.

They were mostly seated already. I looked around and caught sight of the mountainous bulk of Mr. Rand, standing under a tree at one side. He waved to me. I went over to join him.

"Aren't you in the procession?" I asked, shaking hands with him.

"No," he said a little wearily. "I'm getting too old. This is a day for young men."

"I know," I said. "Ben told me that Mr. Brice is to be our next president. I'm sorry Dr. Knox is leaving. I suppose we've all expected it, though, ever since the Guggenheim people adopted us."

"They've let us go again," he said surprisingly.

I looked at him, startled, but before I could speak the orchestra struck up and the academic procession appeared. Dr. Knox in his long black silk robe and brilliant hood, Mr. Brice beside him, somewhat less gaudy; and so on down to the young Bachelors of Arts, rather nude-looking in plain black. I glanced over the audience. I saw several mothers wipe their eyes, and now and then you could hear a male throat clear itself huskily.

It was a great moment for Landover College when Dr.

141

Knox rose and came to the front of the platform, built out over the steps of Mascham Hall.

"I have an announcement to make," he said, "that we have guarded very carefully the last few weeks, so as not to mar in any way this occasion."

I looked at the new president.

Dr. Knox went on in his deep musical voice. Only the soft rustling of green young leaves overhead could be heard.

"Under the will of the late Daniel Sutton of this city, there was bequeathed, to the Board of Visitors and Governors of Landover College, the residue of his estate."

In the surprised and utter silence, his voice grew stronger, and rang out from the Corinthian columns of the old building.

"The residue of Daniel Sutton's estate includes a vast tract of land in the state of New Mexico, formerly used for the raising of stock, and known as El Rancho del Ojo del Espiritu Santo. It has only recently been discovered that this great property, which includes two hundred and fifty thousand acres, is rich in oil and minerals, and is consequently, of what can, at the present moment, only be described as of incalculable value."

A silence as deep as the tomb came over the gay little company there on the college green. The full meaning of enough money to endow Landover College for ever only vaguely struck home.

Dr. Knox went on, deliberately.

"The Visitors and Governors of Landover College, after deliberation, have decided to develop this property for the perpetual benefit of the college. I think, gentlemen—and ladies—that our task, in so far as it concerns the financial support of the College, is over. I feel that this occasion is one of deepest thankfulness, rather than noisy jubilation. May I ask you, gentlemen—and ladies—to stand and bow your heads a moment, in thanks to Providence for its benefits to this ancient institution of learning; and may I ask you further to think reverently a moment of the man who bequeathed us so vast a gift."

I stood like a statue beside Mr. Rand.

I looked up at him, an urgent question in my eyes. His face was calm, but I could see the steely glint in his kindly blue eyes.

"It was Dr. Knox," I whispered. "It was Dr. Knox."

He looked steadily at me without a word.

Dr. Knox was speaking again, but I was thinking of other things.

"How did he know?" I said.

He hesitated only a second.

"I told him," he said then, very quietly. "It was my first violation of professional faith. Sutton left us the ranch as a joke; he thought it was valueless. 'Knox wants land for the college,' he said. 'Here's miles of it.' And Knox was with him when he made that memo. for me. He said he was taking back the land, but he'd find something else for the College."

I watched the brilliant shifting scene, the happy and enthralled faces upturned to the platform, like a person in a dream.

"The revolver in the river?" I whispered.

"Chance—pure and simple. Franklin thought Thorn had done it. I thought till then that he was protecting his father. Franklin simply thought that that's what he'd do with a gun if he had to throw it away—and that's just what his father *had* done."

Dr. Knox's tall slender figure dominating this civilized scene came back to me. I heard him announcing and introducing the new president.

"Mr. Brice," he was saying, "is very young, as you saw in the papers. I have only one word more to say, and it is my advice to all of you. It was said by an English schoolmaster, and it is profoundly true. 'Remember, none of us knows everything—not even the youngest.' "

He lifted his mortarboard with its golden tassel, and returned to his seat. There he sat, erect, courtly, everything a gentleman of Maryland should be. I felt the wave of tenderness and gratitude that swept the audience and burst into a cheer, long and sustained. Even Professor Miggs, who teaches Latin, raised his hat and wrinkled his leathery face.

Mr. Rand and I stood there together. Aunt Charlotte, rocking her chair on the other side of the graduating class, patted her foot as the college orchestra struck up "Landover Forever."